'Enchanting.'

Elliot whispered the word, realising he could quite easily watch Sunainah, listen to her sing, all day long. Who *was* this woman? His gut tightened at the question in a way he hadn't expected. She was attractive. There was no denying that. But the fact *he* was attracted to *her* was a startling revelation and one he didn't really need right now. His life was complicated enough as it was. To add a romantic flavour to the mix could possibly tip him over the edge into insanity.

The past two years had almost broken him, but moving to a new city, new home, new job, was providing a new start for him and his children. That was what he was working hard to accomplish and at no point did a *new* romantic attachment fit into that plan.

Sunainah finished her lullaby and, as though feeling someone was watching, slowly opened her eyes, looking directly into the startled blue gaze of Joshua's father. The moment their gazes held the world around them seemed to stand still…

Dear Reader

THE SECRET BETWEEN THEM is the third instalment in the *Sunshine General Hospital* series. We have loved writing about these strong women who have triumphed over adversity, and Sunainah is no exception. It was a joy to write in her calm yet strong voice, to be a part of her struggles, and to watch how, with the help of Elliot, the new and handsome man in her life, she is able to overcome the pain from her past.

Elliot has been through his own private nightmare, but has managed to set himself back on solid ground once more. Now he just has to figure out how to be a single parent to a three-year-old girl, Daphne, and a two-year-old boy, Joshua. Parenting is never easy, and single parenting is even harder, but with the 'cul-de-sac' crew around him, and the exotic Sunainah, he is able to find the love and support he needs.

The inspiration for Daphne and Joshua came from two gorgeous little children we know, whom we get to spend time with on a weekly basis. These children are only fourteen months apart in age, and at times it's like having twins…but not. It seemed only fair to give single parent Elliot the same joy of raising these two munchkins who are so close in age, and the opening scene of him being in the supermarket, Joshua sick and Daphne missing, is exactly the type of thing that can happen—especially when you feel as though you're only just managing to keep your head above water! Thank goodness Sunainah was on hand to rescue him.

We hope you enjoy THE SECRET BETWEEN THEM.

Warmest regards

Lucy

THE SECRET BETWEEN THEM

BY
LUCY CLARK

First published in Great Britain 2013
by Mills & Boon, an imprint of Harlequin (UK) Limited.
Harlequin (UK) Limited, Eton House, 18-24 Paradise Road,
Richmond, Surrey TW9 1SR

© Anne Clark & Peter Clark 2013

ISBN: 978 0 263 23381 0

Harlequin (UK) policy is to use papers that are natural, renewable and recyclable products and made from wood grown in sustainable forests. The logging and manufacturing process conform to the legal environmental regulations of the country of origin.

Printed and bound in Great Britain
by CPI Antony Rowe, Chippenham, Wiltshire

Lucy Clark is actually a husband-and-wife writing team. They enjoy taking holidays with their children, during which they discuss and develop new ideas for their books using the fantastic Australian scenery. They use their daily walks to talk over characterisation and fine details of the wonderful stories they produce, and are avid movie buffs. They live on the edge of a popular wine district in South Australia with their two children, and enjoy spending family time together at weekends.

Recent titles by Lucy Clark:

ONE LIFE-CHANGING MOMENT
DIAMOND RING FOR THE ICE QUEEN
THE BOSS SHE CAN'T RESIST
WEDDING ON THE BABY WARD
SPECIAL CARE BABY MIRACLE
DOCTOR DIAMOND IN THE ROUGH

These books are also available in eBook format from www.millsandboon.co.uk

To Isabel and Aidan, keep growing to be
as gorgeous and as lovely as you are now.
Pr 13:24

CHAPTER ONE

'It's Rory Preedy's father. He was asking to speak to the head of paediatrics. He actually became quite agitated. I thought I was going to have to call Security.'

'I *am* sorry you had to go through that, Nicole.' Sunainah Carrington shifted the cold tub of yoghurt she was holding to her other hand, wishing she'd had the forethought to pick up a small basket when entering the supermarket. Of course, she had only come in for one or two things but now she was juggling not only yoghurt but bags of vegetables, some apple juice and a self-indulgent block of chocolate. After the day she'd had, she needed the treat…even more so with Nicole's phone call.

Foolishly, Sunainah had thought her day was done, that she would be able to quickly stop off at the shops before heading to her quiet town house to make herself some dinner. Now, though, she would need to head back to the hospital to placate an irate father. The last thing she wanted was for him to create a scene, disturbing the young patients.

Sunainah tilted her wrist to check the time on her watch, accidentally dropping a bag of shallots that had been tucked beneath her arm. 'Oops. Uh…' She bent down to pick up the shallots but dropped the chocolate as well. 'Oh. Uh, Nicole?'

'I help. I help!'

Sunainah looked up at the sound of a little girl's voice and was just in time to see a barrel of arms and legs, clad in a mix of pinks and purples, rushing frantically in her direction.

'Sunainah?' Nicole's voice came through the phone. 'Where are you?'

Sunainah glanced around quickly for the parent of the child, who looked to be about three years old, but could not see anyone nearby who looked as though the little girl belonged to them.

'I help!' the moppet called again, her gaze fixed firmly on the chocolate.

'I am at the grocery store,' Sunainah said into the phone. 'Nicole, I will be there as soon as I possibly can.' Sunainah quickly ended the call and slipped her cell phone into her pocket, removing one of the obstacles, before scooping up the bag of shallots just as the little girl skidded to a halt beside her, rescuing the bar of chocolate. 'Thank you,' Sunainah said as the child handed the chocolate back to her.

'I help.'

'Yes, you are a very good helper.' Sunainah stayed crouched down so she was closer to the little girl's height. She quickly readjusted the items in her arms but once again dropped the chocolate.

The child giggled and picked up the chocolate again, handing it to Sunainah. 'I help!' There was pride in her words but before Sunainah could say another word, the little girl turned and raced off in the other direction.

Concerned that the child was running around the su-

permarket unsupervised, Sunainah quickly stood up and
followed, wanting to make sure the girl was all right.
The store was very busy and the child might run into
someone's shopping trolley or she might be lost and unable to locate her mother. As she watched, she realised
the girl was getting her a basket from the front of the
store. What a clever little one she was.

'You really are a fantastic helper.' Sunainah accepted
the basket from the girl and quickly put her things into
it. 'Thank you very much.'

The girl preened and smiled and wiggled her little
hips from side to side, clearly happy with the praise.

Sunainah once more looked around the store, wondering if there was a distraught mother nearby, trying
to locate her daughter, but there still did not seem to be
anyone frantically searching for a three-year-old. She
knelt down once again and looked at the girl. 'What is
your name?'

'Dap-ne.'

'Daphne?' The child nodded in confirmation.
'What a beautiful name you have, Daphne. My name
is Sunainah.'

Daphne looked very confused at that and Sunainah
smiled.

'Soo-*nen*-nah,' she said slowly, breaking it down.

'Soo-nen-nah,' Daphne immediately repeated.

'Well done. It is a tricky name. Daphne, do you know
where your mummy is? Perhaps I can help you find
her?'

'Mummy's gone.'

'Gone?' Sunainah's eyes widened at this news, worry
for little Daphne immediately piercing her. Daphne's
mother was gone but the child did not seem the least

bit concerned. Perhaps 'gone' in Daphne's world meant something completely different. Perhaps her mother had *gone* down another aisle. 'I do not under—'

Before she had finished speaking, Daphne turned and raced off through the store again, leaving Sunainah barely a moment to collect her basket and follow. She wanted to make sure the gorgeous little girl was indeed safe with her mother.

Keeping her gaze trained on Daphne, Sunainah quickened her pace and when Daphne turned into an aisle, disappearing out of sight, she wanted to run after her. As she turned into the aisle, she almost collided with a staff member, who was wheeling out a bucket and mop.

'Oh. Sorry.'

'You're not the only one, lady.' The teenage worker looked back over his shoulder at the freshly mopped aisle, a look of disgust on his face. 'Gross!'

Sunainah looked around, confused as the teenager wheeled his bucket and mop away, then she spotted Daphne, clinging to the leg of a man who was frantically trying to wipe himself down with some baby wipes. In the shopping trolley next to the man was a crying little boy who, Sunainah belated realised, had recently been sick. The poor mite looked to be no more than eighteen months, perhaps a little older.

All the pieces of the puzzle started to connect themselves. The boy had been sick. The man had sent little Daphne to get help. The stroppy teenage employee had been sent to clean up the mess. Sunainah smiled warmly as she walked towards the man, the scent of disinfectant teasing at her senses.

'It looks as though you have your hands very full.'
She placed her basket on the floor next to his trolley.

'I don't know what happened. One minute I had everything under control and the next the world seemed to explode...or at least Joshua did.' He laughed with disbelief and pulled another baby wipe from the packet and wiped frantically at his shirt.

Sunainah found her lips twitching upwards at the deep, rich sound of his laughter. His blue eyes flashed with mild, confused amusement and she could not help but notice just how handsome this stranger was. 'I do not think that is going to help much. You will end up smelling like a lemon tree.'

'Better than the contents of Joshie's stomach.' The man shook his head then looked at his son who, although his hands and face had been wiped, would still require a change of clothes. 'Poor little man.' He rested the back of his hand on the boy's forehead then frowned.

'Hot?' Sunainah asked as she followed suit. 'Hmm. A little bit.' She looked into the little boy's eyes, noting they were glassy, that his cheeks were very red and his nose was runny. 'A bit of a cold, poor thing.' It was second nature for her to look at a sick child and immediately diagnose them. It was her job, after all.

'He wasn't well before the move but I was hoping he'd be able to fight it off.' The man wiped his hands with another disposable cleaning cloth before holding his hand out to her. 'I'm Elliot.'

'Sunainah,' she offered.

'What a beautiful name,' he instantly remarked, taking the time to really look at her. What he saw captivated him. Not only was her hand soft and supple against his rough palm, not only were her deep brown

eyes filled with a natural joy, but the sound of her modulated voice, so sweet and smooth, was relaxing his
jangled nerves.

'Thank you,' she returned, surprised that he had not
instantly released her hand. It was not that she minded
the cordial handshake but the small spark of awareness that seemed to shoot from his hand to hers before
flooding throughout her body was definitely causing
havoc with her senses. She should say something, do
something to break this strange moment, and it took a
second for her to get her brain back into gear.

'Er…I saw Daphne running around the store,' she
ventured. 'She helped me. Got me a basket.' It appeared
she could only talk in small, stilted sentences. What
was wrong with her? Elliot nodded but did not seem
in any hurry to release her hand. In fact, it seemed he
had forgotten they were still shaking hands. 'I wanted
to make sure she found her parent.'

Elliot's smile increased. 'Thank you. I appreciate
that.' It was as though they were in their own little
world, just for one split second, and as their gazes met
and held once more, Sunainah's heart seemed to lurch
in her chest. What on earth was that? Her eyes widened in surprise.

'I help, Daddy!'

At the sound of his daughter's voice, Elliot seem to
jolt back to the present and instantly let go of Sunainah's
hand to focus his attention on his children. 'Yes. You
helped. You're such a big girl.' Elliot brushed his hand
over Joshua's head. The little boy's crying turning into
more of a constant grizzle, indicating he would soon become highly impatient with his present situation. They
should move. He should put some distance between

himself and this exotic beauty who seemed to have completely captivated him for a few minutes. 'Well, Sunainah...' he nodded politely once more '...thanks again for your assistance.'

'My pleasure.' She bent and picked up her basket, pleased her heart rate seemed to have returned to normal. She should leave it at that and walk away, pay for her groceries and then head back to the hospital to deal with an irate father, but... She angled her head to the side and pointed to Joshua. 'Perhaps I can offer you some further assistance, Elliot. I could watch Daphne while you change Joshua's clothes or at least go to the parents' room and wipe him down.'

A small frown touched Elliot's brow, and she realised that a stranger offering to help him look after his children might be construed as dangerous.

'I promise I am not a lunatic.' Sunainah quickly pulled her wallet from her handbag, showing him her driver's licence. Next to her licence was her hospital identification badge.

'You're a doctor at Sunshine General?' Elliot seemed astonished.

'Paediatrician, so I do have had *some* experience with children.' She smiled down at Daphne, who was watching the exchange between the two adults like someone watching a tennis match.

Elliot looked around at their present surroundings, noticing the way the other shoppers were wrinkling their noses at the stench even the disinfectant wasn't disguising and giving him a wide berth. He needed to get out of the supermarket sooner rather than later and the stunning woman with the Indian-English accent was offering to help him. She was dressed as though she'd not long left the hospital, in a knee-length emerald-green skirt and cream-coloured shirt, her long black hair pulled into a low bun at the nape of her neck. Tidy, professional…perfect.

Elliot gave his head a little shake, needing to get his thoughts back on track. He was in 'Daddy Hero' mode. He needed to contain the situation, to fix things, to get his life and his children back under control, back on track, not stand in the middle of a supermarket aisle with a sick child, ogling the woman before him, who he realised was going to be one of his new colleagues. He probably should mention that but right now his son required attention, and Sunainah's offer of help would indeed expedite the situation.

'Thank you, Sunainah. I'd appreciate the help. First off, why don't we head to the checkout, then we can find the parents' room.'

'I know where it is.'

'Do you have children of your own?'

'No. I am not a parent.' They walked towards the checkout, Daphne more than happy to slip her hand into Sunainah's free one. She smiled down at the girl. 'You are very friendly, little one.'

'Sometimes too friendly.' Elliot shook his head as they lined up at the checkout. 'The whole "stranger-danger" concept is too much for her to grasp at the moment, which does pose a few concerns.'

'Of course,' Sunainah agreed, trying to hide a smile as the woman with a large shopping trolley filled with groceries sniffed the air then turned to stare at Elliot and his son. She was ahead of them in the checkout line but after assessing the situation immediately insisted Elliot go before her.

'Thank you.' His words were polite and his smile was warm and inviting and Sunainah watched with interest as the woman's reaction instantly changed to one of delighted compliance. A blush tinged her cheeks and she smiled brightly at him. Elliot's charming smile had made this woman completely flustered.

Had she looked that way when she had first seen him smile? He *was* a very good-looking man, with his tall stature, his straight nose and square jaw, and his eyes really were the most dazzling blue. She also liked the way his curved lips highlighted a small dimple in his left cheek. His dark hair was peppered with grey at the sides but that only made him look more distinguished, or perhaps it was the way he carried himself, with pure confidence mixed with purpose.

It was not every day she stood and openly ogled a man, and as he quickly put his groceries onto the small conveyor belt at the checkout, she gave herself a mental shake, clearing her thoughts and focusing on the people around her. It was then she noticed Daphne had unpacked her basket of items and put them onto the conveyor belt with her father's.

'Oh, no. These are a separate transac—' she started to say to the teenage girl, who was already scanning a few of her items.

'It's fine.' Elliot's smile encompassed her. 'It's the least I can do after your offer of assistance.'

'Well…' Sunainah realised it was not the time or the place to make a scene, and as her friend Reggie always said, 'Why stop a man from being chivalrous? Just say "Thank you" and move on.'

'Thank you, Elliot. That is very kind.' Sunainah returned his smile and bowed her head for a moment in a gesture of added thanks.

Once they were free of the supermarket, she led the way to the parents' room, Daphne still holding her hand and Elliot pushing Joshua in the trolley behind them. The room was equipped with three baby-changing stations, chairs for parents to sit in, toys for young children to play with, a sink, a microwave and a television. There was also a parent toilet cubicle with one large and one small toilet, specifically provided to make it easier for both mums and dads.

'Do you have a change of clothes for him?' Sunainah asked as Daphne was instantly captivated by the toys.

'I do.' Elliot pulled a bag out of the trolley and opened it up. Nappies, clothes, drinks, fruit snacks and other paraphernalia required for taking children out was contained inside.

'Did you also pack a change of clothes for yourself?' She smiled as he lifted the grizzling Joshua from the trolley and placed him on the change area.

'Unfortunately, no. Must remember that in future.'

'Daddy. Daddy.' Daphne came running over to him, jumping up and down and crossing her legs, a pained expression on her face. 'Toilet.'

Elliot groaned. 'It never rains but it pours.'

Sunainah chuckled. 'Go. I can deal with Joshua.'

He seemed to pause for a moment, looking at her as though he was amazed a complete stranger was really willing to help him out. 'Er...right. OK. Thanks.' With that, he reached for his daughter's hand and quickly entered the parental toilet cubicle.

'Right, Master Joshua. Let us get you settled,' she stated, and after finding what she needed in the bag quickly changed him with the experience of a woman who did this sort of thing several times a day. By the time Elliot emerged with a happy and relieved Daphne by his side, Joshua was making himself comfortable in Sunainah's arms, resting his head on her shoulder.

Elliot stopped and stared at the sight they made. Joshua, with his mop of blond hair, resting his head close to Sunainah's exotic skin was a contrast of delight. She was gently patting his back, singing a soft lullaby in her native language. Her eyes, such a deep, rich brown with long dark eyelashes, were closed. She swayed gently from side to side, lulling his son to sleep.

Who was she? Of course he knew her name and where she worked, and it was clear from the evidence before him that she definitely had a way with children, especially as Joshua detested being held by strangers, but apart from that she was like some sort of angel, sent from heaven right when he'd needed her most.

Even Daphne, who did everything at the fastest speed possible, simply stood there and watched the stunning woman sing Joshua to sleep.

'Enchanting.' Elliot whispered the word, realising he could quite easily listen to Sunainah sing all day long. Who *was* this woman? His gut tightened at the question in a way he hadn't expected. She was attractive. There was no denying that but the fact *he* was attracted to *her* was a startling revelation and one he really didn't need right now. His life was complicated enough as it was. To add a romantic flavour to the mix could possibly tip him over the edge into insanity.

The past two years had almost broken him but now the move to a new city, new home, new job was providing a new start for him and his children. That's what he was working hard to accomplish and at no point did any romantic attachment fit into that plan.

Sunainah finished her lullaby and, as though feeling someone was watching, slowly opened her eyes, looking directly into the startled blue gaze of Joshua's father. The moment their gazes held, the world around them seemed to stand still, just as it had when they had shaken hands. Sunainah was highly aware of her heart pounding, the sound reverberating in her ears as Elliot's gaze momentarily dipped to encompass her mouth.

She swallowed, surprised she was unable to look away from him. His gaze met hers once more and he opened his mouth as though to say something but then seemed to change his mind. His mouth looked perfect and a flash of desire pulsed through her as she wondered what it might be like to feel the pressure of that perfect mouth pressed against her own.

The thought shocked her. It was so unlike her. She was not the sort of woman to ogle strange men, nor was she the sort of woman to simply stand there and stare, but for the first time in her life she was unable to control her unbidden reaction to this handsome stranger.

Perhaps she was acting out of character because two of her closest friends had recently married, and seeing them both so happy had started her wondering whether she would ever have the courage to find happiness. Perhaps it was simply that at times she was very lonely, wishing she had someone to share those little inconsequential moments with. Perhaps it was that Elliot appeared to be a nice, kind man and that had sent her imagination into overdrive. Her experience with nice, kind men—with the exception of her father—had been few and far between. Besides, Elliot was no doubt happily married and was surprised at the strange language in which she had been singing.

'Sing a song. Sing a song,' Daphne demanded, running to Sunainah's side and tugging on her skirt. The distraction seemed to snap both adults out of their trance and Elliot immediately came over and scooped Daphne into his arms.

'Uh…' Sunainah quickly cleared her throat, forcing her mind to work, to click back into 'normal' mode rather than the one it was presently in where she seemed to be highly aware of every little nuance about Elliot… Elliot *who*? She did not even know his surname and yet here she was, pondering what it might be like to spend hours just staring into his eyes, eyes that were the most glorious shade of blue she had ever seen.

'Uh…Elliot, do you have any child-strength paracetamol?' She forced herself to look away as she asked the question, pleased her mind had finally clicked back into 'useful' mode. She still felt highly self-conscious and aware of every small move he made as he reached into the bag and pulled out a bottle of liquid paracetamol.

'Here.' Elliot quickly drew up the correct dosage of paracetamol in the provided syringe then carefully squirted it into the sleeping Joshua's mouth. The child swallowed dutifully but didn't stir in Sunainah's arms.

'That should help him to settle even more,' she murmured, glancing up with a small smile on her lips. It quickly disappeared as she realised just how close she was to Elliot and even though he still did not smell the best, the warmth exuding from him seemed to surround her like a comfortable blanket.

What was it about this man that was making her behave so uncharacteristically? She needed distance from this little family so she would help him get his children settled in his car, collect her belongings and then head to the hospital, and she would probably never run into Elliot or Daphne or little Joshua ever again. She ignored the instant pang of disappointment and pushed it aside. The sooner she was away from his captivating presence, the better.

She forced herself to look away from his enigmatic eyes. 'Uh...perhaps if you show me the way to your car, I can carry Joshua so you do not need to disturb him any further.'

'OK.' With that, Elliot put Daphne into the shopping trolley and wheeled it out of the parents' room. He headed down the travelator to the basement car park and Sunainah followed, the sleeping Joshua in her arms.

It felt warm and wonderful, holding the little boy so close. Poor little thing. Since becoming a paediatrician, she had loved so many of her little patients, watching them grow strong and healthy. Nothing gave her more pleasure...but one day she would love a few children of her own. She shook her head, not wanting to think about how that would never happen. No, she must be content to love the children in her care at the hospital. That was her vocation.

Being an only child had not been much fun and it had not been until she had started medical school in Sydney that she had formed a lasting friendship with three other women, who now felt more like sisters to her.

The bond between herself, Mackenzie, Reggie and Bergan had only grown stronger over the years and now, with all four of them working together at Sunshine General Hospital on Queensland's Sunshine

Coast, Sunainah loved meeting with them, enjoying lunch or breakfast or just a quick coffee, depending on their varying schedules.

They were people she could rely on and that had been proved six weeks ago when Sunainah's father had finally, after over a decade of being ill, died peacefully in his sleep in the nursing home.

She rubbed her hand on Joshua's back, drawing comfort from the sleeping boy as she once more felt a pang of loneliness. Even though her father had been in the nursing home for the past two years, his death had still left an enormous, gaping chasm in her life. At the insistence of her friends, Sunainah had moved from her one-bedroom flat, which had been close to the nursing home, to a lovely two-storey town house, and was now living next door to both Mackenzie and Bergan.

There were four town houses in a small cul-de-sac and now only one of them was vacant…although now she thought about it, she did remember Bergan mentioning it had recently been rented so perhaps there would soon be new neighbours for her to meet.

Elliot pulled a set of car keys from his pocket and pressed the button to unlock a nearby vehicle, the car's indicators flashing along with a short beeping sound. 'Here we are.' He opened the back passenger door for her and smiled politely. 'Are you all right to put him—?'

'It is fine. I can manage.' She kept her own smile equally as polite and was relieved when he stepped away to the rear of the car to stow his purchases.

Daphne kept saying over and over, 'I help!'

Once both children were strapped securely into their car seats, little Joshua's forehead not feeling so hot as it had earlier, Sunainah closed the door and walked around to where Elliot was holding her shopping bag out to her.

'Thank you.' She accepted it gratefully.

'No.' He exhaled slowly. 'Thank *you*, Sunainah. You've been a real lifesaver.'

She smiled, unsure what else to say. 'It was nice to meet you.'

'Likewise.' He stood there, staring at her for a moment, drinking her in. A small bubble of excitement started to build in his gut, knowing he would no doubt see her tomorrow when he started his first shift in the paediatric department at the hospital. He should probably tell her and was just about to when her phone rang.

'Sorry,' she said as she dug her cell phone from her handbag. She checked the caller identification. 'It is the hospital. I had better go. I have an irate parent to deal with.'

'Sounds like a barrel of fun.' Elliot flicked his car keys from one hand to the other.

She chuckled then indicated the phone, which was still ringing, and took a few steps away from him. 'Goodbye…Elliot.'

'Until next time, Sunainah,' he remarked as she turned away, connecting the call.

'I am sorry, Nicole. I was unavoidably delayed,' he heard her say as he watched her walk away. Why he stood there, watching until she was out of sight, half wanting her to look back at him, half wanting her to disappear from view as quickly as possible, he had no idea.

Finally, he turned and walked to the driver's side of his car. 'Until next time.' Elliot couldn't help the excited smile that touched his lips at the thought.

CHAPTER TWO

SUNAINAH SAT AT the nurses' station situated in the centre of the very bright and colourful paediatric ward at Sunshine General, working her way through a mound of case notes, reviewing the previous night's notes. At least, that was what she was trying to do, except her mind kept flicking back to her encounter with Elliot.

Until next time. Those had been the last words he had spoken to her. What had he meant by that? Was he planning to bump into her at the grocery store another time? She smiled. That would be nice but how would he accomplish such a thing?

Until next time. Sunainah sighed and closed her eyes, remembering all too clearly just how wonderful his smile had been. It had been clear his children loved him and vice versa. Although the situation had been quite disastrous with Joshua being sick and Daphne running around the store, he had not snapped or yelled at them. Indeed, when they had been in the parents' room he had been quite calm and attentive towards Daphne when she had needed to go to the toilet. Yes, a good father.

'Who more than likely is married to the equally good mother of those children,' Sunainah muttered with a sigh, and opened her eyes. It was not the first time she had told herself this fact…but why, if he *was* happily married, had he stared at her in such a way? Was it usual for a man to simply look at another woman with that much intensity and *not* be interested in her?

'Mother of which children?' Nicole asked as she walked back into the nurses' station, handing Sunainah a much-needed cup of coffee.

'Er…nothing.' Sunainah sat up a little straighter in her chair as she sipped the coffee. 'Perfect. You are a lifesaver, Nicole. Thank you.'

Nicole sat down beside her, putting her own coffee cup onto the desk and picking up another set of notes. There was a note clipped to the front, and she pointed it out to Sunainah. 'Rory Preedy's file. Bethany said she'd be available to talk to the father this morning at ten o'clock.'

'Good.' Sunainah read the note from the social worker. 'Poor little Rory. No wonder he is finding it difficult to get better. He does not want to go home.'

Nicole nodded and edged closer, lowering her voice. 'Do you suspect child abuse?'

'No, not at all.' Sunainah sighed. 'I suspect it is more a case of a father pressurising his poor son to get better quickly because he expects Rory to be as robust as himself. He might be under a lot of strain at work and does not know how to deal with having a sickly child. Rory was ten weeks premature and now, at the age of three, has spent more time in hospital than his parents probably expected. Hopefully, with Bethany's assistance we can help Mr Preedy to accept his son needs a bit longer to recover than most children.'

Nicole nodded. 'I hope you're right.'

'When I spoke to him last night, I will admit, it was

a little difficult to get through to him but…I have a sense that behind all his bluster he is a man who is very worried about his son but has no idea how to show it.'

Sunainah reread the note from Bethany before making a note in her cell phone. 'Ten o'clock. I shall need to excuse myself from the heads of department meeting. OK. Shall we try to get through this work before the new paediatrician arrives? It would be nice for everything to be up to date so I can show him around without—'

'Say no more,' Nicole interrupted and handed Sunainah the next set of case notes for them to review.

The two women worked together for the next five minutes, engrossed in their work. While the ward itself was quite noisy, with the sounds of children talking and laughing, they were used to it so when a deep male voice spoke from the other side of the desk, both women looked up, startled.

'Excuse me. I was hoping you could help me.'

Sunainah stared at the man, blinking one slow, long blink to ensure she was not dreaming. 'Elliot?'

He smiled at her. 'Hello again, Sunainah.'

She frowned. 'Is everything all right? Joshua? Has his fever spiked?' Sunainah stood, worry clearly etched on her features, but as she did so she realised Elliot was wearing a white coat. Not only that, he also had a hospital identification badge hanging from a lanyard around his neck.

She was trying to process why on earth he was dressed that way when she saw a smile cross his lips and realised, belatedly, that she had spoken her thoughts out loud. She put her fingers over her mouth as though to retract the words but it was too late.

'I'm a doctor.' He nodded. 'Paediatrician, to be exact. The new Sunshine General paediatrician and I'm pleased to report that Joshua is much improved.'

'Until next time.' Sunainah whispered the last words he had spoken to her and slowly shook her head from side to side as the penny finally dropped. She looked at his hospital badge and saw his surname was Jones.

'Dr E Jones.' Sunainah spoke the words quietly, re-calling the paperwork she had previously signed, ap-proving the appointment. It had been only days after her father's funeral and Sunainah had much preferred to assuage her grief by hibernating at the hospital, work-ing as much as she could. That was why she had not remembered that the *E* on Dr Jones's application had stood for Elliot. It was why she had not put two and two together and come up with four.

She now remembered reading his CV and being im-pressed. She had been delighted the hospital board had finally agreed to provide funding for another paediatri-cian as they had been incredibly understaffed for the past year.

'That's me. Elliot Jones.' He paused for a moment. 'Look, I know I should have said something yesterday and I did try but…well, it was busy and…'

Sunainah straightened her shoulders, managing to recover some of her composure. 'I understand, Elliot. Your son was not well and you clearly had other things on your mind…as well as on your clothes.' Her lips twitched and she was rewarded with a bright smile from him.

She immediately put out a hand to the desk for sup-port because the instant he turned his full-megawatt smile in her direction, her knees immediately began to buckle. Was he aware his smile could be classified as lethal? Sunainah closed her eyes for a brief moment before once more taking in the badge and white coat. Elliot was a doctor! Was this why he had trusted her so quickly with his children? He had known the instant he had seen her identification that they would be working together.

Until next time.

'Sunainah?' Nicole, standing beside her, watching the two of them rather intently, cleared her throat.

'Oh, yes. I apologise. Elliot, allow me to introduce my colleague, Nicole Tada.'

Elliot stretched out a hand towards Nicole and shook her proffered hand. Nicole immediately checked his left hand for a wedding ring and when she didn't find one she asked bluntly, 'So you're not married?' At Elliot's raised eyebrows Nicole continued. 'Sorry to be so blunt but, quite frankly, I have a few young agency nurses who love to flirt. It will make my life easier if you *are* married.'

Elliot shook his head. 'Sorry, Nicole. I'm a widower.' His voice dropped to a more reverent tone and Sunainah noticed the sparkling look in his eyes dulled a little as he said the words that were never easy to say. 'My wife passed away the day after my son was born.'

'Oh, Elliot.' Sunainah's heart instantly went out to him as the memory of cradling the small blond boy as he slept flashed through her mind. 'I am so sorry to hear that.'

'That's why Joshie is so precious to me. Daphne, too.' Elliot smiled pointedly at Sunainah. 'She has her mother's get up and go. Always wanting to help.'

Sunainah's smile was tinged with sadness as she remembered the little girl's words yesterday. *Mummy's gone.* The poor lamb. She probably had no real memory of her mother. 'She is very good at it.'

'Hang on.' Nicole held up her hands as though calling for a time-out. 'How do you two know each other?'

'Uh…well—' Sunainah was about to answer when there was a loud crash then a bang, followed by an almighty cry from one of the ward rooms. Elliot and Sunainah headed instantly in the direction of the disturbance, a shared room of four boys, but when they arrived it was to find two boys of about seven years old sprawled out on the floor, both of them crying.

'It was *his* fault.' One of the other boys, still safe in his bed, instantly pointed. Sunainah quickly took in the situation, with the overturned bedside tables, jigsaw-puzzle pieces everywhere and the contents of two plastic cups on the floor.

One of the boys had a cast on his leg and was having difficulty getting up off the floor. Elliot immediately scooped the boy up and carefully deposited him on his bed, while Sunainah helped the other boy up.

'Are you all right, Matthew?'

Matthew was still crying as she lifted him onto his bed so she could inspect him better. She glanced across at where Elliot was talking to Dean, ensuring that his cast was still intact and that there was no other permanent damage done.

'We were doing the p-p-puzzle together,' Matthew said between his tears, his voice hiccupping. 'And he put a piece in the wrong side and I said it was wr-wr-wrong but he…he…'

'Shh,' Sunainah soothed. 'It is all right.' She glanced over her shoulder and realised that Nicole, who had followed them in, was calling a few other nurses in to help with the clean-up.

'But now the pieces are wet,' Dean added, his own sobs blending with Matthew's.

'It will be all right,' Sunainah told him. 'It is just water and it is only on one or two pieces that are wet. We will get them dry for you.' She looked at Matthew. 'Now, can you lie back on the bed for me, please? I need to check your bandage is still in place.'

Matthew did as he was told, and when Sunainah checked his abdominal bandage she found the dressing was still firmly in place. 'Thankfully, you have not pulled your stitches out, which would not have been good.' Even though her voice was firm, she smiled at him.

'May I suggest,' Elliot said as he settled Dean back into bed, 'that we set the puzzle up in the playroom and after both of you have had a little rest and Nurse Nicole has dried out the wet pieces, you can start again. That way, you don't need to lean across the beds or accidentally knock over the bedside tables.' As he spoke, Elliot righted the tables and wheeled them back to the end of each boy's bed.

'Good idea, Dr Elliot. In fact,' Sunainah continued, 'I will even come and help you to get the puzzle started again.'

'You'll really come and help us?' Dean asked, and Sunainah smiled at him, straightening her shoulders.

'I am an expert at doing jigsaw puzzles.'

'Really?' Matthew's eyes were wide.

'Yes. My father and I used to do a new one every few weeks. It was great fun.'

Elliot caught the past tense in Sunainah's words and

as he watched her a little more closely he noticed a moment of sadness cross her face. It was the same sadness
he'd seen yesterday and from the way she'd needed to
swallow, he realised her pain was very recent.

'Do you still do them?' Dean wanted to know.

'I think that's enough excitement for now,' Nicole
interrupted in her best nurse-knows-best voice. She
glanced at Sunainah, who smiled gratefully, knowing
the nurse had timed her interruption to perfection.

'Nurse Nicole is right.' Sunainah pulled Matthew's
sheets up to tuck him in a bit more. 'I know it is almost
eight o'clock in the morning but you have all been up
and wide awake since half past five so now will be a
good time to rest.'

'That goes for you two as well,' Nicole added, tuck-
ing in the other two boys in the rowdy ward room.

'Ward round will be starting soon,' Sunainah told
them, 'so you must all be on your best behaviour. Once
it is over, we will all go to the playroom and start the
jigsaw.'

'Yes!' Dean pumped his fist with delight and Elliot couldn't help but smile. It was nice to see the boys
enjoying an activity that wasn't about the latest computer game.

'Let us leave Nicole to settle the boys,' Sunainah
suggested, motioning towards the door. 'She is much
better at it than you or I will ever be.'

'Thank you,' Nicole remarked with a wide grin.
'With five brothers and three children of my own, I do
consider myself something of an expert.'

'And while we are waiting for the other consultants
and registrars to arrive...' Sunainah turned to look at
Elliot '...I will give you a quick tour of the ward.'

'Sounds like a plan,' Elliot replied.

'And the first thing I will show you is the cupboard where we keep our white coats.' Sunainah grinned as they headed towards the doors that led to the paediatric ward. Just off to the side was another doorway, which opened up to reveal a closet. 'It was a decision made quite some time ago that the doctors would not wear white coats because there was the possibility it might frighten the children. A hospital can be a very scary place for someone so young and this way we at least make it a bit more happy for them.'

As she spoke, Elliot removed a few things from the pocket of his coat and dutifully took it off and hung it up. 'Done. Next.'

'Ah…' She crooked her finger, indicating he should follow her. 'The next thing you must see is the kitchen. We have a microwave, toaster and refrigerator if you want to bring your lunch from home and, of course, we have tea- and coffee-making facilities.'

As Elliot looked at the kitchen, he nodded. 'I'm pleased to see you have your priorities straight. Every new doctor should be shown the way towards the near-est source of coffee.'

Sunainah laughed at his words, the sweet sound washing over him like a soft, comfortable blanket. Didn't she have any idea how the laughter brightened her dark eyes, washing away any hint of repressed sad-ness?

'Do you need a cup before rounds?'

Elliot shook his head. 'I'm doing all right at the mo-ment, thanks.'

'Excellent. So…on with the tour.' She showed him where the photocopier was, how they filed the paperwork and a few other things. 'And this,' she said, opening a door at the end of a short corridor, 'is my office.'

'They tuck you away down here?'

'I was offered a larger office but it was not on the ward and I would much rather be doing my work here, nice and close to the patients.'

'Quite right, too,' he agreed. 'I would have chosen the same.' He looked around the room, walking in, looking at the generic prints on the wall and the large umbrella plant in the corner. 'Did you decorate it?'

Sunainah smiled and reviewed her office décor. 'No, I did not. This was how I inherited it from my predecessor.'

'I thought you might have some pictures up that your grateful little patients have drawn for you.'

'Those brilliant masterpieces we usually put on the picture wall in the ward so everyone can see and admire their handiwork. Oh, but I do have...' She walked around to her desk drawer and pulled out a battered necklace made from dried macaroni pasta. 'As you can see, it is a little worse for wear.'

'You've actually worn it?' Elliot came around to inspect it, noticing the way Sunainah's fresh floral scent wound its way around his senses. It wasn't an exotic scent but one that was understated and very pretty. He liked it.

'Of course. A little boy called Patrick made this for me. He was only three years old at the time but now he has just turned thirteen.'

Elliot watched her eyes light with happiness as she spoke of her past patient. 'What was his story?'

'He was mute.'

Elliot raised his eyebrows in surprise. 'Not something you come across every day.'

'No. Patrick had been traumatised. He had witnessed the death of his father and after that he closed up his words tight, like a clam shell. His mother was distraught and it was thought that the best place for Patrick was at the hospital. He barely interacted with the staff and three days after he came in here he went missing. We searched everywhere and eventually I found him. He was hiding in one of the cupboards in the playroom.'

'Poor little fellow.'

Sunainah nodded. 'Yes. I will never forget the look on his face, seeing him there, completely terrified. Instead of trying to coax him out, I sat down next to him and started to play with some of the toys. It took well over an hour for him to feel secure enough to come out of the cupboard and after that he was like my little shadow. He would only eat if I was around. He responded better to his sessions with the psychologist when I was there.'

'And I'll bet you were a hectic registrar with a massive workload and yet you still made time for him.'

'But of course.' Sunainah's words were matter-of-fact, as though she had not even thought of doing otherwise. Besides, she knew firsthand what it was like to be pushed aside when a parent could not cope with enormous life changes. The instant those dark, personal thoughts entered her mind she forced herself to lock them away again.

'Patrick was my patient. He needed me. One day I found him in the playroom, sitting by himself, making this necklace. When I asked him if it was a present for his mother he shook his head. Then he came and placed it around my neck.' Tears began to well in her eyes and she quickly looked away, putting the necklace back in the drawer.

'A perfect moment.' Elliot's words were soft and filled with empathetic understanding.

Sunainah raised her gaze, surprised. 'Yes.' Elliot understood?

'We have so few of those in our lives, Sunainah. It's important to recognise them when they come along, which you clearly did as you've kept that necklace, broken and battered as it is. It's not just a necklace given to you by a little patient, it's a symbol of love. A love that was not only given from Patrick to you but also a constant reminder that what you do, the way you choose to care for your patients, is important.'

'Yes. I needed to be there for him, so he had someone to lean on.'

'Exactly.' Elliot pointed to the drawer. 'I'll bet that on days when things go wrong, when nothing seems to work out the way you want, you come in here, close the door and put that necklace on.'

Sunainah nodded, surprised Elliot seemed to understand her so completely. How odd. No man, not even Raj, who had been her fiancé, had understood.

'I know because I have something similar.' He reached into his pocket and pulled out a small piece of smoothed wood. On it were the childishly shaped letters *D-A-D*. 'Daphne made this for me just before we left Melbourne to come here. She gave it a kiss, then put it into my hand and then kissed me on the cheek. She wrapped her little arms around my neck and said, "I love my daddy."'

Elliot looked down at the keepsake in his hand before closing his fingers around it and shoving it back into his pocket, trying to keep his voice calm and controlled. It wouldn't do for him to get overly emotional in front of his new colleague.

He shrugged one shoulder. 'I needed to have it with me today, to remind me why I've uprooted my children and moved them away from everything and everyone they've ever known.'

Sunainah watched him for a moment. 'You are still not sure you have done the right thing?'

'No, I know I've done the right thing but I also know it isn't going to be at all easy.' He turned away and walked to the small window that overlooked the doctors' car park. 'Sometimes we need to walk the more rocky path.'

'It makes us stronger,' she ventured, agreeing with him. They both remained silent for a moment before Sunainah spoke softly. 'May I ask you a question?'

Elliot shrugged one shoulder but didn't turn to face her. 'Sure.'

'Why did you openly tell Nicole that your wife had passed away? Your marital status is rather irrelevant as far as your job is concerned.'

He exhaled slowly then turned to face her. 'Because I loathe gossip. I'd rather the staff know right from the get-go that I'm a widower with two young children. No speculation. No whispers of *Is he single?* or *I wonder if he's ready to date?*—the latter of which I received at my last hospital *ad nauseam.*'

Elliot shook his head with frustrated sadness. 'My wife had breast cancer, diagnosed four months into her pregnancy. She refused to terminate the pregnancy and although the doctors started chemotherapy, the cancer was too aggressive. Joshie was born five weeks premature. Marie died the day after he was born.'

'I am so very sorry, Elliot.' Sunainah's words were soft and filled with empathy.

He shook his head and spread his arms wide. 'I don't like the fact that I've been a widower for almost two years. I don't like the fact that I'm a single father who felt so smothered by my wife's family that I moved to the Sunshine Coast in order to get away from them. I don't like it that Joshie has been sick and that Daphne ran off in the supermarket yesterday and I didn't even have a clue she was missing.' Elliot raked a hand through his hair. 'Anything could have happened to her.'

'But it did not.' She paused. 'I am presuming you were successful in enrolling them in a daycare centre?'

'Yes. My new neighbour told me the one she uses is good so I called and the woman there was very accommodating and willing to take both the children immediately.'

'That is wonderful news. Where are they going?'

'A place called Grandma Liz's daycare centre. It's not far from the hospital, which is good because if they're ever sick or I'm needed in a hurry, I'm close by.'

Sunainah smiled. 'I do know the place. My friend's daughter goes there and she loves it.'

'Well, that's another good recommendation.' He pushed his hand through his hair then shook his head. 'I keep telling myself it's just one step at a time. Deal with things as they happen—which was all I could do yesterday. And everything would have taken even longer to sort out if you hadn't offered to help.'

'It was my pleasure.'

'Yesterday only brought home to me that I have no

clue what I'm doing as a parent or how I'm going to cope.'

Sunainah smiled, her voice soft and sweet. 'And then you put your hand into your pocket and you find that small piece of love with your name on it. It is a love you can hold, can grasp when you need it most. You love your children, Elliot. I could see as much yesterday. You will figure everything out. I am sure of it.'

He looked at her with a hint of scepticism. 'How can you be so certain? So positive?'

'Because you are talking about it. Most men do not talk of their feelings in such a way, plus it is easy to see just how much your children love you.' Her cell phone rang and she quickly pulled it from the clip on her belt. 'You will make friends and so will the children and soon you will find your feet again.' She nodded with a certainty Elliot found easier to believe than the lectures he'd been giving himself.

'Is it ward round time, Nic—' Sunainah stopped, then sighed as she listened to what Nicole was saying. 'All right. Page Bethany to see if she can come now instead of at ten o'clock. Have William start the ward round. I will be there directly.'

'Problem?' Elliot asked as she ended the call.

'A patient's father is unhappy,' she remarked as they exited her office. 'I spoke to him last night and thought I had soothed his ruffled feathers but he has come back this morning.' Sunainah shook her head, a frown creasing her perfect forehead.

'What is it?'

'Pardon?'

'Your instincts are telling you something, Sunainah. What is it?'

'I do not think he likes female doctors. It does not seem to matter what I or any of the nurses tell him, he does not think we are looking after his son adequately.'

'Ah. I know the type. If you'd like some assistance, I'd be more than happy to offer mine.'

Sunainah thought for a moment before nodding. 'A fresh perspective might be good.'

'Then lead the way, Dr Carrington. I've got your back.' Elliot nodded then winked at her, his voice filled with an honest promise.

As Sunainah walked towards the nurses' station, feeling Elliot's strong, warm and comforting presence behind her, she was quite dumbfounded. No man had ever promised to support her in such a fashion, his tone indicating he might be someone she could actually come to trust. In fact, no man had ever winked at her like that—jovial yet determined. Elliot Jones, a man she barely knew, was willing to help *her*.

What had she done to deserve such attention?

CHAPTER THREE

AT THE NURSES' station, several people were gathered—consultants, registrars, dieticians, interns and even a few medical students. William, her more-than-capable registrar, who had almost finished his paediatric training, caught her gaze. Sunainah nodded once, giving him the all-clear to begin the round.

'I demand to speak to someone who knows what they're really doing around here.' The booming male voice came from one of the side rooms and Sunainah instantly stiffened, turning in that direction. She would have to walk over there and deal with Mr Preedy yet again.

Right now, it was the last thing she wanted but, she reminded herself, she was a strong woman who protected her patients, even if it was from their own parents. Besides, she did not appreciate people making a scene in her ward, not only upsetting the patients but making the staff feel uneasy. Arrogant, overbearing men were her least favourite people to deal with and a shiver from other times she had heard such a tone ran down the back of her spine.

Elliot was standing just behind her and as she paused for a moment, ensuring her memories remained repressed, Elliot's comforting words washed over her again.

'I've got your back,' he reiterated, his words firm and unyielding.

Sunainah swallowed and turned to look up at him, which, she realised belatedly, was a very large mistake. Elliot was much closer than she had realised and as she stared into his eyes, surprised to feel comforted by his presence, she tried with great difficulty to ignore the way his spicy scent invaded her senses, momentarily making her forget everything.

'Er...thanks,' she whispered, then swallowed over her suddenly dry throat. Why was she so aware of him? It was odd and confusing and—

'I'm here, Sunainah,' Bethany, the paediatric social worker called as she closed the door behind her. 'Nicole caught me at the perfect time.'

'I am glad you could make it.' Sunainah indicated Elliot. 'This is Elliot Jones, our new paediatric consultant.'

Bethany quickly shook hands with him but anything she might have said was cut off by the loud, blustery voice coming from the private room near the end of the corridor.

'Why does he still have these tubes going into him? Why isn't my son getting better?'

'I see Mr Preedy is starting early today,' Bethany remarked drolly.

'It is unfortunate,' Sunainah replied, handing Elliot Rory Preedy's case notes. William had set off on the ward round, taking the gaggle of medical students, interns, registrars, nurses and consultants with him. Having so many people in the ward along with Mr Preedy's booming voice cutting through the usual calmness the staff strove hard to promote was increasing Sunainah's agitation. She needed to get this situation under control as soon as possible and she most sincerely hoped Elliot was going to assist her, as he had promised.

'Shall we?' Nicole asked, pointing in the direction of Rory's room.

'Yes,' Bethany replied. 'We'd best rescue the poor nurse he's yelling at before he tears her to shreds.'

Elliot closed the file and walked closely behind Sunainah. 'I have an idea how to handle this man.'

'Really?'

'Just…please don't be offended if I seem a bit different. Sometimes the only way to deal with a man like Mr Preedy is to speak his language.'

'Anything for Rory. The patient comes first,' she stated as they all paused outside Rory's private room before Nicole opened the door.

Elliot pushed past the three women and strode firmly into the room, flicking Rory's case notes open. He didn't look at Mr Preedy, didn't look at the young nurse, who took the opportunity to escape through the open door like a frightened bird flying the coop.

'Hello, Rory.' Elliot's voice was controlled but not as loud as Mr Preedy's. 'I'm Dr Elliot Jones and I'll be monitoring your progress today.' He looked down at the notes then back to Rory. 'You've just turned three years old, is that correct?'

Rory, surprised to see another man in the room, glanced once at his father then at Sunainah. Sunainah nodded encouragingly and Rory mimicked her action, nodding his head.

'My own son, Joshua, is almost two years old. He

likes to play with cars and trucks. Do you like cars and trucks?'

This time Rory didn't look at anyone before he nodded his head but kept his eyes trained on Elliot.

'Excellent.' Elliot turned to Nicole. 'Perhaps we can get some small cars and trucks in here for Rory to play with?'

'I'll get it organised, Doctor,' Nicole replied, her voice calm.

'Good.' Elliot put the opened case notes at the end of Rory's bed, flicked over a few pages, then nodded. 'I see the treatment for your urinary tract infection is coming along just nicely.' He still hadn't looked at Mr Preedy and when Sunainah glanced at the parent, it was to see him scowling, unappreciative that his rant had been interrupted.

'Who are you? This is my son,' Mr Preedy blustered.

Elliot exhaled harshly, as though he was annoyed with the interruption. He still didn't look at Mr Preedy but instead focused on checking Rory's drip. 'I'm Dr Elliot Jones.' He finished what he was doing, then finally raised his gaze to look firmly into the other man's eyes.

Sunainah blinked, feeling as though she were watching a scene from an old Western, the two men staring at each other in a stand-off. Elliot was almost half a foot taller than Mr Preedy and much broader in the shoulders. She was reassured by the strength he exuded. He had told her he was going to try speaking Mr Preedy's 'language' and it appeared Elliot was winning.

After a good fifteen seconds had ticked by, Elliot held his hand out towards the father. Mr Preedy waited a moment before accepting the hand. The handshake was more like a firm clasp with no up and down shak-

ing going on at all. 'I'm one of the paediatricians here
at Sunshine General and I'll be joining Dr Carrington
here…' he nodded politely towards Sunainah '…in caring for your son while he's in our ward.'

'You must be new.' There was a slight hint of accep-
tance in Mr Preedy's tone.

'I am, and as I have just joined Dr Carrington on this
case, I must say from what I've read in young Rory's
notes and from what I see here…' Elliot waved a hand
in Rory's direction '…his treatment has been exem-
plary.' He still kept his words brisk, clipped and very
much to the point.

'All I can really do is reassure you that everything
is progressing exactly as it should be and if everything
continues to go without a hitch, if Rory is able to rest
effectively and relax so his body isn't too stressed out
from being pressured to get better, then he should be
ready for discharge by the end of the week.'

Matter-of-fact. That was his attitude. No nonsense.
Take charge. That was the persona Elliot was portray-
ing for Mr Preedy, that he was the doctor in charge and
he would make sure everything ran smoothly from now
on. Then he said something that surprised her. His tone
remained the same but the look in his eyes changed to
one of shared comprehension. 'Mr Preedy, I can see
you're a caring father who only wants the best for his
son. I understand that completely, being a father myself.'

'Er…yes.' Mr Preedy shuffled his feet, clearly uncomfortable but not willing to back down. Sunainah
instantly felt sorry for the man. It was evident he was
having difficulty showing exactly how much he did care
for his son and she hoped that somehow, some time he
would come to know it was all right to show affection

towards Rory. 'I had…er…just thought he would have
been better by now.'

'I'm sure Dr Carrington has explained the treatment
to you and the main factor that will assist with Rory's
immediate recovery is not to be around loud noises.
Having some cars and trucks brought in for him to play
with will help ease his boredom and maintain a sense
of calm. Hopefully, by tomorrow morning we'll be able
to remove the catheter and Rory will be able to spend
some time in the playroom with a few of the other children. I understand it might sound old-fashioned and
slow but at the moment rest, relaxation and time will
play an important part in Rory's recovery.'

'That's what *she* said,' Mr Preedy remarked, a scowl
returning to his features as he jabbed a finger in Sunainah's direction.

Elliot smiled brightly. 'Then you have nothing to
worry about. Between Dr Carrington and myself, as
well as the nurses caring for him, we'll have Rory up
and about in no time at all. The two of you will be lying
on your living-room floor, playing cars and trucks and
building with blocks, before you know it.'

At these words Bethany suddenly had a coughing
fit as she tried to cover the bubble of laughter that had
escaped her lips. Clearly the image of Mr Preedy lying
on the floor and playing with his son was too much for
the social worker to bear.

Elliot closed the case notes, gently ruffled Rory's
hair and looked pointedly at his watch. 'Good heavens.
Is that the time?'

The suggestion did the trick as Mr Preedy also
glanced at his watch, his eyes widening with shock.
'I'm going to be late for work.' He looked at Rory then

at Elliot then back at his son. He took a step closer and placed a hand on the boy's shoulder. 'Keep getting better, son. Your mother will be here shortly.' His tone was still clipped but didn't have any of the previous volume. Without looking at any of the women in the room, he turned and strode out.

No one spoke for a few seconds, the air filling with a sense of incredulity. There was the strange sense that everyone should clap but they all refrained, not wanting to excite or upset Rory. Bethany spoke first, her tone calm yet filled with admiration. 'Good job, Elliot.' She grinned at him before exiting Rory's room.

'I'll go see about those toy cars,' Nicole told them, winking at Rory as she followed Bethany out.

Sunainah moved closer to Rory's bed and gently folded back the bed covers to reveal more of the little boy's face. 'It is OK now,' she reassured him with a smile. 'You can start to get better.'

Rory seemed to sigh with relief at this news, as though he had just been waiting for someone to tell him he could get better. 'Dr Elliot and I, along with Nicole, will all take good care of you and make sure your father and mother understand what is going on.'

The boy nodded once then looked at Elliot. 'Dr Sunainah's right,' Elliot remarked, his tone exactly like the one he had used with Joshua yesterday. Caring, understanding, compassionate. 'And once some of the tubes are removed, you'll be able to join in the fun in the playroom.'

This brought a smile to Rory's face and when Nicole returned with some toy cars and trucks, his smile got bigger.

Elliot wheeled over the bedside table, and Sunainah

helped Rory to sit up a little higher. The boy instantly grasped one of the cars in his hand. The two doctors stood there, playing cars with Rory for a few minutes while Nicole checked Rory's catheter and drip.

'I hope that big truck does not come and bump my car,' Sunainah remarked, indicating the truck Elliot had in his hand. Rory's eyes twinkled with delight as Elliot moved his truck towards Sunainah's car and smashed into it, making Rory giggle with glee.

Sunainah sighed, pleased to see the young boy smiling once more. She glanced across at Elliot, surprised to find him looking at her. He smiled at her and winked once more as though to say, 'I told you I could help.' And he had. He had done what he had said he would do. This was a good step in the right direction when it came to trusting her new colleague.

'I'll stay with him,' Nicole stated, looking from Elliot to Sunainah, both of them quickly shifting their gazes to look at the nurse. 'You two can go and catch the end of the round—that way you can introduce our new superhero to the masses.' Nicole grinned at Elliot before he stood, said goodbye to Rory and then held the door open for Sunainah to precede him.

'Nicole is right,' Sunainah said, trying to ignore the way her heart was beating a little faster than before. She was sure it had nothing to do with the cheeky wink Elliot had given her. Honestly, he was just a colleague and while he might be a very good-looking colleague, he was still just a colleague…and she would do well to remember that.

'Right about what?' he asked as he handed Rory's file in at the nurses' station.

'You are a superhero.'

Elliot grinned but didn't try to deny it. 'At your service, Dr Carrington.' He performed a sweeping bow, making her laugh out loud. It was a wonderful sound, soft and light and causing his gut to tighten. Her smile was bright, her eyes alive with laughter and he had to admit that at that moment he couldn't believe how incredibly beautiful she looked.

'Then, Dr Superhero, let us join the ward round and perhaps discover what other superpowers you possess,' she remarked, laughter still twinkling in her eyes.

'Lead the way, my trusty sidekick.'

Sunainah laughed again as they left the nurses' station, walking towards the crowd still moving from one bed to the next, reviewing the patients. 'I do not think I am a sidekick,' she said, 'but I am happy to have you as a part of my team.'

Elliot nodded, his smile still bright. 'And I'm happy to be here.' Even though he'd basically said the words in order to be polite and keep the mood upbeat, Elliot realised that for the moment he actually meant it.

That night, after an exhausting day of meetings and paediatric clinics, not to mention spending time in the playroom with Matthew, Dean and a few of the other boys, doing a jigsaw puzzle, Sunainah was glad to finally get back home.

As she drove into the small cul-de-sac she passed a removal truck that was just leaving. Outside the first town house a few large packing boxes were stacked on top of each other. It was then she remembered her friend Mackenzie had told her someone new had moved in, and here was the proof.

Although Sunainah was tired after an emotionally

exhausting and mentally draining day, especially with the meetings she had been required to attend, she knew it would be better to go and introduce herself to her new neighbours sooner rather than later. Mackenzie would no doubt be organising cul-de-sac dinners and get-togethers before too long and it would not be right for Sunainah not to know her new neighbours.

Parking her car, she climbed out, pulling some energy from thin air as she walked towards town house number one. The front door was open and she could hear girlish giggling inside, the delightful sound making her smile. What was it about a child's uninhibited laughter that managed to soothe her soul? Every day when she heard it at work she knew she had chosen the right profession.

She knocked on the open front door. 'Hello?' She stepped over the threshold, hearing the sounds of grown-up laughter following that of the children's. Male and female. It appeared they had a family living here for a while, which would be nice for Ruthie, Mackenzie's six-year-old daughter.

'Hello?' she called again, venturing farther into the house, following the sound of the voices.

'Oh. Sorry,' a man's voice called out from near the top of the stairs, a voice that was...vaguely familiar. Sunainah frowned but continued walking towards it. A moment later Elliot appeared before her and quickly came down the stairs, a big smile on his face.

'Sunainah! Mackenzie just told me that we're going to be neighbours.' He was now standing beside her at the foot of the stairs.

'Hi, there,' Mackenzie said, looking down at both of them as she slowly descended the stairs. 'I didn't realise Elliot was also a doctor until a few minutes ago and then when he told me he worked in paediatrics, well...' Mackenzie shrugged and flicked her blond hair over her shoulder. 'What else was there to say? He's going to fit in perfect with our little cul-de-sac family, don't you think?

'Er...yes.' Sunainah could not think of anything more to say right at that moment but it did not matter because Mackenzie was on a roll. 'Anyway, Elliot,' she said, smiling politely at him, 'please, come on over when you're ready and we'll have dinner together. Unpacking boxes can be exhausting and hunger-inducing work.' Mackenzie grinned at Sunainah. 'You're coming, too,' she ordered. 'Bergan and Richard will be there too.'

'And Reggie?' Sunainah could not resist asking. Mackenzie was such an organiser and it was clear she was in her element tonight.

Mackenzie shook her head. 'She's on call tonight. Besides, it's just the cul-de-sac crew.' She laughed. 'I love how that sounds.' She turned and angled her head towards the top of the stairs. 'Ruthie. Come on, gorgeous girl. We'll go and get things ready for Daphne and Joshua's visit.'

'I go, too,' Daphne said, appearing at the top of the stairs next to Ruthie.

'Wait there, sweetheart.' Elliot instantly rushed up the stairs to collect his daughter while Ruthie barrelled down the stairs with all the expertise of a girl of six.

'I help, Daddy. I help.'

'It's fine with me,' Mackenzie stated. 'Joshua can come, too. I don't mind.'

'Yay!' Daphne ran through to the downstairs bedroom, calling to Joshua. A moment later the little boy came running after his sister, not really sure what was happening but not wanting to be left out either.

'All righty, kids. Let's go.' Mackenzie scooped Joshua up into her arms and reached down for Daphne's hand. The little girl was more than happy to go along, following Ruthie eagerly. 'See you two in about ten minutes,' Mackenzie called over her shoulder, and before Sunainah could blink she was standing in Elliot's new residence, all alone with him.

'She's certainly an organiser,' he remarked.

'Ruthie or Mackenzie?'

Elliot chuckled. 'Both?' He looked at her, his smile warm and sincere and inviting. Sunainah found it difficult to look away, even when the smile started to disappear. The silence seemed to stretch between them and the spicy scent she had noticed about him earlier in the day still surrounded him, teasing at her senses.

She tried to think of something to say, something to break the mounting silence building between them, but, much to her chagrin, her mind remained blank. It was not the first time it had happened since she had met Elliot Jones and it was clear that if she was going to work effectively alongside him she would rapidly need to find a way to avoid instances such as these.

'I've never been part of a cul-de-sac crew before.' Elliot finally broke the silence between them, his voice a little husky, as though he had just confessed a great secret.

'Neither have I.' *Come on, Sunainah. Pull yourself together*, she chastised herself.

His eyebrows rose. 'How long have you been a part of this…crew?'

'Only a few months. Richard, he is married to Bergan, used to live at number three, or his parents did. Then when they decided to move closer to Richard's sisters, number three was up for sale. I was ready for…a change.'

'Sounds as though it all worked out perfectly.'

'Yes.'

'And now you're part of the *crew*.' He said the last word as though it really were some kind of secret club, his eyes alive with excitement. She could not help returning his smile.

'Apparently so.'

He pointed to her clothes, belatedly realising they were the ones she'd been wearing at the hospital. 'Have you just arrived home from work?'

'Yes. I wanted to come and welcome you before I lost myself in the mound of paperwork I have brought with me from the hospital.'

'Thank you. It's nice to be prioritised before the rigorous, never-ending paperwork.' He jerked his thumb over his shoulder towards the kitchen. 'Can I offer you a cup of tea? Coffee?' He stopped and snapped his fingers. 'Sorry. Scratch the coffee. I haven't unpacked my coffee machine yet.' He turned and walked towards the kitchen, and Sunainah, although she knew she should no doubt make her excuses and leave, followed him.

'A cold drink perhaps?' He opened the fridge as he spoke. 'I can offer you milk, milk or tap water.' Elliot grinned at her over his shoulder.

'Thank you but I am not thirsty. I had a coffee meeting with Bethany before leaving the hospital.'

'About Rory?'

'No. Ever since you allayed Mr Preedy's concerns this morning, probably by making him think there was a male at the helm of his son's treatment plans, we have all had a much more agreeable day, especially little Rory. I have a feeling his health will vastly improve now.'

'Pleased to hear it.'

'Bethany and I were discussing young Matthew. His mother is having a difficult time dealing with Matthew's mood swings so we were brainstorming practical alternatives for her to employ at home once Matthew is discharged.'

'Good.' He nodded as he poured himself a glass of tap water. 'Let me know if I can be of any assistance.'

'Thank you, Elliot.'

'It's good to see that as head of department. You really do have your finger on the pulse. You're not so busy worrying about budgets and cost projections that you don't have the time to really be a part of your patients' lives.'

Sunainah smiled. 'I must admit that at times it can be a bit of a juggling act but this is my second year in the position and I finally feel as though I am coping better.' She paused and thought over his comments. 'Have you been in a department where the director cared more about budget projections?'

He laughed without humour. 'I can name quite a few places I've worked that are like that.'

'What about you? Were you involved in the running of the department back at your previous hospital? I did read your résumé,' she confirmed, 'but it was a long time ago and a lot has happened since then.'

'I'm hurt you don't have it memorised,' he joked, and noticed a momentary flash of confusion touch her rich brown eyes before they twinkled with delight, her lips curving into a smile. Hmm, perhaps he should tease her more often if that was how it made her look. He drank his water, more to distract himself from staring at her beauty than because he was thirsty.

'Seriously, though, I used to be head of department, but that was before Daphne was born. After that, Marie started getting very tired. At first we thought it was postnatal depression and then, before we knew it, she was pregnant with Joshua and even more signs and symptoms presented themselves that had nothing to do with PND.' His voice trailed off and he placed his empty glass into the sink, staring at it for a long moment.

Sunainah had not missed the change in his voice when he had spoken of his wife. The emotions and struggles the two of them would have faced, and to have a young child thrown into the mix as well as a second pregnancy…it would not have been an easy time.

'It is clear you miss her.'

He nodded and met Sunainah's gaze. 'Yeah, I do. I always will because she was the mother of my children and the love of my life but…it's time.' He turned to face her, leaning back against the cupboards, crossing his arms over his chest. 'It's time for me to stand on my own two feet, to be a good parent, to move the three of us forward as our own family unit because back in Melbourne I…I felt like I was constantly wading through the quagmire of my past.'

'Things were…not good?'

Elliot shook his head sadly. 'No. They were not good.' He slowly exhaled then looked across at Sunainah, standing next to a stack of three packing boxes. Most of his furniture had been delivered the previous day but with starting a new job and Joshua being sick he simply hadn't had the time to do anything with it.

'The last two years have been fraught with friction and I found myself caught in quite a toxic atmosphere. I battled on for a while, as you do, thinking that things would settle down, that they'd get better, but they didn't and it was the children who were suffering the most.'

'Toxic?'

He shrugged one shoulder. He didn't particularly feel like going into details, not after the hectic day they'd both had, but he also knew he couldn't leave it there. Besides, his first impressions of Sunainah were that she was someone he could trust, so he plunged in, deciding to give her some basic facts about his past.

'Marie's parents felt I wasn't…coping all that well after my wife's death and, well, to cut a long story short, they took preliminary steps to file for custody of my children.'

'Oh, no!' Sunainah put her hand up to her mouth, completely shocked. 'Elliot. I am so very sorry.'

'Thankfully, I still have full custody of my own children now, hence the main reason for the move.'

'Understandably. I do hope they are able to settle in with little fuss.'

'I'd say they're off to a good start as apparently they had a wonderful day at Grandma Liz's. Ruthie was there after finishing school for the day and she told me that Daphne and Joshua were both laughing and playing well with the other children when she arrived.'

'A glowing report.'

'Yes.' Elliot smiled. 'Six-year-olds can be very open and honest, and I'm sure if Daphne had been sitting in a corner, crying, Ruthie would have reported it.'

'Oh, yes. She is very good at reporting on events is our Ruthie.'

'Our Ruthie?'

'I am one of her godmothers.'

'One of?' He was clearly intrigued.

Sunainah smiled at the question. 'Bergan, Reggie and I are all godmothers to Ruthie, therefore, she is "ours". You will meet Bergan tonight at dinner.'

'But not Reggie because she's not part of the cul-de-sac crew,' he pointed out with that telltale teasing light in his eyes.

Sunainah chuckled. 'Exactly.'

'The four of you are good friends?'

'Yes. Mackenzie, Bergan, Reggie and I have all been close friends since we met at medical school in Sydney.'

'And now you're all here, working in Maroochydore on Queenland's Sunshine Coast at the same hospital?'

She shrugged. 'It may seem odd how things have worked out but I would not have been able to cope during the past few years without their constant help.'

'Your father?' he guessed, wondering how she would react to such a personal question. He watched as her brow creased into a small frown and was amazed at how lovely she still looked. It was odd, this sensation of being attracted to another woman. He hadn't planned it and he certainly hadn't asked for it, and yet along with the interest he felt towards his new colleague there, at the back of his mind, was also a nagging sense of guilt.

He had pledged his love to Marie, his beautiful wife, the mother of his children…but now she was gone and he was left feeling like an adolescent again, out of his depth and unsure what to do next. Making friends, getting to know Sunainah a little better seemed like the logical course of action to take, but now that he'd asked his personal question, would she answer it?

'How did you—?'

'You mentioned you *used* to do jigsaws with your father. I had hoped the reason you weren't still doing jigsaws with him was because he was off travelling somewhere, enjoying his life, but when I saw that mixture of sadness and grief in your eyes, a look and feeling I know all too well, I guessed at the real reason.'

She nodded and looked down at her feet for a moment. 'He passed away just after Christmas.'

'I'm sorry.' He watched her for a second. 'Some days I bet you wonder if you'll ever get used to saying those words out loud.'

'It still sounds wrong. I cannot believe I will never see him again.' She shrugged a shoulder, still unable to meet Elliot's gaze properly. 'My father was sick for quite some time and eventually he had to go into a nursing home.'

'That wouldn't have been an easy decision for you to make.'

'No. It was not.' She sighed and swallowed over the lump in her throat.

'How long was he in the nursing home?'

'Almost two years, and every day he seemed to deteriorate just that little bit more.' She shrugged one shoulder. 'So at least I had time to prepare myself for the inevitable.'

'It's still not easy, though.'

She was pleased Elliot did not offer her platitudes but appeared to clearly understand her sensitive emotions. 'No.' Finally, she met his gaze. 'I doubt it will ever be easy.'

Elliot nodded. 'I know people often say "I know how you feel" but I actually *do* know how you feel, and while it wasn't your spouse who passed away, it sounds as though you were very close to your father.'

She nodded. 'Yes. We were very close.'

'And your mother?'

'She passed away before we came to live in Australia.'

'You were in India?'

'No.' Sunainah shivered uncomfortably. Even the mere mention of India caused her heart to feel heavy and oppressed. 'England.'

Elliot realised Sunainah had most certainly experienced her fair share of grief. It was clear there had been a lot more to her life to have sculpted her into the woman who stood before him.

'I was fortunate to have a lot of time with my father and when, with regret, it was necessary for him to live in the nursing home, I found a small place close by so I could see him as much as possible.'

'And you did lots of jigsaw puzzles.'

Sunainah held his gaze. He truly did understand. 'Yes. Then, after he passed away, there was no reason for me to be living so far away from Sunshine General. The town house was up for sale and as I knew the owners I decided to buy it, to try and give myself a complete change, much the same as you have done.'

'And now we're both part of the cul-de-sac crew.'

'Yes. It is strange having so much room to spread things out but I am slowly getting used to it.' She smiled but it didn't reach her eyes and he could still hear the sadness in her tone. She patted the boxes beside her, wanting to lighten the atmosphere. 'So if you need any help unpacking, I am quite qualified.'

'Good to know.' Elliot uncrossed his arms and

pushed away from the sink, taking a few steps in her direction and leaning on the same stack of boxes, his close proximity causing her heart rate to increase instantly, her body to flush with heat, her mind to turn completely blank.

'Fresh starts.' He glanced down at her mouth, noticing the way her lips parted as her breathing increased. 'For both of us.'

'Er…yes.'

He met her gaze once more and when she saw an interested spark light up his hypnotising blue eyes, she found it difficult to suppress the confused excitement that pulsed around her body.

Elliot reached out and gently trailed the backs of his fingers down the side of her cheek, marvelling at how perfectly soft and smooth her skin was, just as he'd known it would be.

'For both of us,' he reiterated, his words slightly more pointed than before.

CHAPTER FOUR

'SO HOW ARE things going?' Mackenzie asked Sunainah one morning about a week after Elliot had burst into her life. They had been out for their early morning jog, something they tried to do together at least once a week if their schedules allowed, and were just returning to Sunainah's place for a nice cool drink when Mackenzie asked the question.

'How is what going?' Sunainah opened the fridge. 'I have pineapple and guava juice.'

'Sounds great but stop trying to change the subject.' Mackenzie tucked her feet beneath her on the chair and leaned on Sunainah's kitchen table. 'You have my undivided attention.'

Sunainah laughed. 'What are you talking about?'

'Elliot!' Mackenzie straightened and spread her arms wide before accepting the glass of juice Sunainah had poured. 'What's been happening between you and Elliot?'

'Nothing is happening. We are colleagues and neighbours.'

'Well, there was definite sexual tension between the two of you last week when we all had dinner together.'

'There was not.' She shied away from her friend's words. 'He is a nice, kind man.'

'Exactly.'

'Who is nice and kind to everyone he meets,' she pointed out as she sat opposite Mackenzie and drank the cool liquid.

Mackenzie sipped her juice, a cheeky grin on her face. 'So you're telling me you haven't even...dreamed about him?'

Sunainah almost choked on her juice at the words. She coughed, which only made Mackenzie laugh. 'A-ha. You have dreamed about him.'

'They were just dreams. I do not understand why you are so excited about it. I have dreamed about many people over the years. Like the Queen of England, she was in a dream of mine once. And Ruthie, your daughter. She was in a dream once.' She spread her arms wide. 'Dreams are just dreams. They do not mean anything.'

But even as she said the words, images from her dreams of Elliot flashed through her mind. The two of them gazing deeply into each other's eyes, Elliot closing the distance between them, cupping her face with his gentle hands before he put them both out of their misery and pressed his mouth to her quivering lips.

Mackenzie giggled. 'Sure, sure. You keep telling yourself that, Carrington. Maybe one day you'll believe it.'

'You are a crazy lady.' Sunainah laughed at her friend.

'All I'm saying is that it's good. It's been over five years since Raj the rat left you despondent and alone.'

'Do not call him that.' Sunainah felt compelled to

defend him, even though what Mackenzie had said was true.

'I call 'em as I see 'em and Raj *was* a rat.' Mackenzie sipped her drink again, shaking her head and tut-tutting. 'The way he was insisting your father be shoved out of the way into a nursing home after you were married? That's the sign of a wrong 'un.'

Sunainah nodded, agreeing with Mackenzie. She felt no real ill will towards Raj, only that she had had a lucky escape. Breaking off their engagement, even though he had left her with more questions than answers, had been painful at the time but now she was grateful.

'Early-onset dementia can be managed without round-the-clock nursing care. My father was more than settled in my home and, yes, I have to confess I was extremely hurt when Raj suggested shoving my father away, but he simply was not able to see things the way I did.' She shrugged. 'At any rate, I did not marry Raj—'

'Thank goodness,' Mackenzie interjected.

'—and instead we moved here to Maroochydore, closer to you and Bergan.'

'So I should be thanking Raj the rat for breaking your engagement?'

'Yes, and so should I because coming here, being close to you and Bergan and Reggie, well, I would never have been able to get through these past few years without you all. You are the best and most supportive friends a girl could ever ask for.'

'Aw, shucks. You're gonna make me cry.'

'Friendships are important,' Sunainah continued to point out as she finished her drink and stood, stacking her glass in the dishwasher. 'Which is why it is going to be far better for me to see Elliot as a friend, regardless whether I occasionally dream of him or not.'

'What about…the other thing?' Mackenzie asked softly after a moment.

Sunainah held her friend's gaze. 'The other thing Raj discovered? About my past?' She shook her head and closed her eyes, doing her best to block out the thoughts and force those horrible memories back into their box. 'It is another reason why there can never be anything but friendship between myself and Elliot.'

Which was a shame because whenever Elliot winked at her or smiled at her or stood close to her, she found herself wanting to do nothing else except stare into his amazing blue eyes, eyes she knew she could lose herself in for ever if she was given half the chance.

'But—' Mackenzie began, but Sunainah held up her hand.

'No.'

'I will help. So will John and Richard and Bergan and—'

'No.' Sunainah calmly held up both hands, indicating Mackenzie should not continue with the subject. 'I…I cannot. I am not… I do not want to…' She sighed. 'I am not ready.'

'Fair enough.'

'However, we should not sit here for too much longer or we will be at risk of chatting our day away.'

'True. Lucky John has the day off, which means I've left him a long list of jobs to do.' Mackenzie grinned as she unfolded her legs and stood, moaning a little as she stretched. 'Ooh, I'm getting old.'

Sunainah laughed and said goodbye to her friend, before racing upstairs to have a shower and dress. 'Elliot

Jones is a nice man and a good father,' she told herself as she flitted around her home, picking up different manila folders and other bits of paper and putting them carefully into her bag. 'He has children who need him and no doubt has no room in his life for any sort of romantic entanglement. Neither, for that matter, do you. You have a busy department to run, you have patients who need your love and attention. That *is* enough for you.'

Sunainah sighed as she stood at the bench and quickly drank a cup of coffee. She had never been the type of woman to go on lots of dates, usually only agreeing to one whenever Reggie set it up. Sunainah would go, she would be polite, allowing herself to enjoy a man's company for one night before she told him that they could never be anything but friends. It drove Reggie insane.

'You deserve happiness, Sunainah,' Reggie had said more than once.

'I am happy, Reggie,' she would reply.

'There is a sadness in your eyes that will never leave you. I know that. I know what happened to you, remember, and from everything you've told me, it wasn't your fault. You shouldn't be punished for a barbarian's mistake.'

'And yet it is my burden to carry.' Sunainah had looked firmly at her friend. 'Leave it. Please, Reggie?'

'All right,' Reggie had grumbled. 'But it's still not fair.'

'No,' Sunainah whispered into the quiet of her kitchen. 'It is not fair.' Neither was it fair that she had finally met a man who intrigued her, who made her feel soft and sweet and feminine just by smiling at her. No doubt Elliot Jones had no thoughts about her of the romantic kind, no thoughts beyond the fact that she was simply another of his colleagues.

He seemed to enjoy working alongside her and she had to remind herself that he was just as bright and smiling with her as he was with Nicole or Bethany or any of the other female staff on the paediatric ward. She should not confuse politeness with flirting.

Sunainah finished her coffee, picked up her bag and walked through the lounge room, stopping to look at the family portrait hanging on the wall. It was something she had done every day since her father had passed away, to stop and say 'See you later' to her parents.

Both of them were smiling in the photograph, which had been taken not long before her mother's illness had revealed itself, an illness that had ended up changing all their lives. For a while, though, they had been happy together, the Indian woman and the Englishman with their teenage daughter.

She shook her head and brushed a hand down her skirt. It would not serve any purpose to dwell on the past, to dwell on things she could not change. What did matter now was getting to the hospital before she was late for ward round.

Sunainah almost forgot her thermos of coffee and headed back into the kitchen to pick it up. Mondays were often too busy for her to have a proper break so eating at her desk while completing paperwork had become somewhat of a habit.

One week. She still could not believe she had known Elliot and his children for a week. Well, just over a week given their first meeting in the supermarket had really been the first time they'd laid eyes on each other. She sighed as she walked out to her car, thinking of little Daphne, so desperate to be helpful, and poor little Joshua, not feeling at all well.

The dinner they had shared last week at Mackenzie's house had been filled with a lot of laughter and quite a bit of bonding. Ruthie had played well with Elliot's children, keeping them well amused and entertained, leaving the adults to enjoy their time crowded around the dining table, sometimes talking over each other and at other times laughing at the idiosyncrasies that went hand in hand with hospital life.

Bergan and her new husband, Richard, had been married for four months, and where Sunainah had often thought that she and Bergan would remain the two un-married out of their group of four, now it looked as though it would just be her. Mackenzie and John had been married for almost nine months and were talking of perhaps giving Ruthie a sibling or two to dote on.

'She's certainly good with your two, Elliot,' Mackenzie remarked as she gathered the plates and took them into the kitchen.

While the conversation seemed to swirl around her, Sunainah could not help but to sneak small glances at Elliot throughout the informal evening. He really was a very handsome man. There were no two ways about it, with his dark hair and perfect blue eyes. But it was the way he genuinely loved his children that spoke most to her heart.

'Daddy, Daddy, Daddy,' Joshua whimpered as he came toddling into the room, holding his hands out to-wards his father. As soon as Elliot picked the boy up, Joshua put his head on his father's shoulder and snug-gled in.

'Getting tired, little man?' Elliot asked, then glanced

at his watch, surprised at how late it was. 'And with good reason. It's way past your bedtime.'

He stood from his chair as Ruthie and Daphne came into the room. Sunainah watched as the little three-year-old rubbed at her eyes, clearly tired as well. What had surprised Sunainah most was Daphne. Seeing her brother firmly settled in their father's arms, she ran to Sunainah and held her arms up.

'Soo-*nen*-nah?'

'Aww. How gorgeous is that?' Mackenzie remarked when Sunainah instantly obliged and picked her up.

'It's settled, then,' Elliot said, smiling at her. 'You have been chosen to assist with the Jones children's bedtime routines. Come along, Dr Carrington. Help me get my children to bed.' Elliot had spoken without concern or compunction for how his words might be interpreted. He had called a cheery goodnight to all gathered, as though he'd been a part of their group for years, then headed towards the door, holding it open for Sunainah and Daphne.

'After you, pretty ladies.'

Daphne giggled. Elliot winked. Sunainah blushed.

They headed out into the cool March evening. 'I'm so glad I decided to move here. The weather is far nicer than in Melbourne.'

'You have missed Queensland's tropical summer. Sticky, humid and hot with a lot of rain. Now the weather is not too bad, although I must warn you that it can still get very hot during the middle of the day. The children must always have their hats and sunscreen on.'

Elliot nodded. 'Duly noted. Thank you.' He opened the door to his new residence and headed inside, side-stepping the boxes scattered here and there.

'I meant to ask you before, Elliot. Are you just renting or did you buy?'

Elliot looked at the walls and nodded. 'I bought this place. I was determined the move here would work, and it will.'

'Yes. Very determined.' She could not help but smile at him, liking his display of courage. As she watched him carry Joshua through the house, the little boy already asleep on his father's shoulder, Daphne started to snuggle in further.

'Are you getting sleepy, pretty girl?' Sunainah asked, and Daphne nodded. Then, as though realising she had Sunainah all to herself, she lifted her head, her brown eyes alive with happiness.

'You help me, Soo-*nen*-nah. You help Daphne.'

Before Sunainah knew what was happening, she was helping the three-year-old get ready for bed, Daphne clearly knowing her night-time routine.

'Brush teef. Do night nappy. Put on nightie. Story time. Song time then sleep time.' Daphne ticked the things off on her little fingers, looking very adult and quite serious. Sunainah could not repress the smile that instantly touched her lips.

After they had ticked the other things off the list, they were finally up to song time. Sunainah sat in the large rocking chair, the only other piece of furniture in the room besides Daphne's bed. While the little girl snuggled warmly into her, Elliot came into the upstairs room.

'I can take it from—'

'Shh,' she whispered, before continuing with her soft song. It was the lovely Indian lullaby she had sung to Joshua the first day they had met. Elliot did as he was told and when she'd finished, he pulled back Daphne's bedcovers, making it easier for Sunainah to put the sleeping three-year-old into her bed.

'You really do have a lovely voice,' he said as they headed downstairs.

'Thank you.'

'What do the words mean?'

'They are a way of expressing gratitude and appreciation to a specific person.' Sunainah's eyes twinkled with a teasing light. 'Hence the "you" tagged on at the end.'

Elliot stared at her for ten seconds before he noticed the small smile tugging at the corner of her mouth as she walked towards the front door. Stunningly beautiful, sensitive and funny. No wonder it was becoming increasingly difficult for him not to think about her.

'I meant the lullaby, not the words "thank you",' he said with a soft, rich chuckle, the sound settling over her like a warm and comforting blanket.

'Oh. The lullaby.' Her smile brightened and she nodded. 'They say to rest in your dreams and to know that tomorrow will bring happiness and peace to your soul.'

'How enchanting.'

Sunainah nodded, waiting for Elliot to open the front door. Instead, when he simply stood there, staring at her with an odd expression on his face, one of surprised happiness—or so she hoped—she started to feel a little self-conscious.

'Sunainah, please allow me to offer you my…gratitude and appreciation for your assistance this evening.'

She smiled at his words. 'You are most welcome.'

Then, before she had gathered any idea of what he

might do next, Elliot leaned across and brushed a soft and lingering kiss to her cheek.

Sunainah's eyes widened in surprise.

'I think I'm going to like working and living here.' He nodded. 'The people are…very nice.'

She felt stunned, unable to think of anything in reply, and after Elliot opened the front door, bidding her farewell once more, Sunainah walked on numbed legs back to her place, constantly caressing the place on her cheek where his lips had left their mark.

She touched her fingers to her cheek once more, even though it had been a week since that light kiss. There was no way it could mean anything other than a gesture of friendship as he had already confessed that his wife, Marie, had been the love of his life. It was good that he was moving forward with his life, especially where his children were concerned, but she had seen the look in his eyes when he had spoken of Marie. He had been deeply in love with his wife, of that she was certain, and just because he was making changes to his life, it did not mean he was looking for any sort of romantic attachment.

'He is nice and good and kind to everyone,' she told herself as she finished packing her handbag and picked up her car keys. If she did not stop staring off into space, recollecting the past, she would continue to make herself late for work.

'So you can stop this silly nonsense, the silly dreams. It can go nowhere and you will only end up hurting yourself if you persist with these schoolgirl fantasies.' She continued to speak sternly to herself as she headed towards the garage, pressing the remote-control button

for the roller door. 'You are his colleague and his friend
and that is all.'

'Ah...Sunainah! Good. You haven't left yet. I'm so
glad I caught you.'

Elliot's voice came from the other side of her garage
and as the door continued to rise, so Sunainah's spirits
lifted up towards the heavens at the sight of him. So
much for all the lectures she had just given herself. At
the first sound of his voice she was right back to where
she had started when she had first opened her eyes that
morning. Her smile brightened as she caught sight of
the man who was plaguing her dreams. He looked even
better in real life.

'I'm having car trouble. Mackenzie's agreed to take
the children to the daycare centre for me and I was hoping I could get a lift to the hospital with you.'

'Of course.' Sunainah unlocked her car and held the
passenger door open for him.

'Thanks. I've already called the car-hire place and
they've said they'll send someone out to deal with it
later today.'

Sunainah slipped into the driver's seat, trying not
to be so aware of everything about him. The way his
clothes seemed to have been tailor-made to fit his perfect body. The way his spicy scent filled the car, intoxicating her senses. The way his deep, rich voice washed
over her as he talked so easily, in such a friendly way
to her. It was difficult to keep her mind on the task at
hand, especially when he smiled at her as though she
were his own personal angel, helping him out in his
time of need.

How on earth was she supposed to drive now? She
stared at the steering-wheel for a moment while Elliot

buckled his seat belt. It was no good. Rational thought was not returning. She closed her eyes for a moment, willing logical thought to return.

'Sunainah?' Elliot's deep voice snapped her back to reality, and she quickly looked at him. 'Are you all right?'

Hearing the concern in his voice made her feel as though she was a fraud. 'Yes, yes. I am fine.' She started the engine and reversed out of the garage, pressing the button on the remote to lower the roller door afterwards. 'Er...do you have any idea what might be wrong with your car?'

He nodded. 'The alternator. John's already been out and had a look and agrees with me. He's rostered off today so at least someone will be around when the mechanic comes.' Elliot shook his head. 'Honestly, I couldn't have asked for better neighbours and the fact that we're all doctors and work at the same hospital is most definitely a bonus.' He nodded.

'Most definitely,' she repeated. She forced herself to concentrate on driving and not on the fact that his presence seemed to fill her small car and overwhelm her senses. So busy was she, concentrating, that she slowly began to realise that neither of them were speaking. She glanced at Elliot then quickly returned her attention to the road when she realised he was frowning deeply.

'Is something wrong?' she asked, and was pleased when his frown immediately lifted.

'No. No. Not really. As I said, I'm glad to have moved into the cul-de-sac and am now a member of the cul-de-sac crew. It's highly fortuitous.' Although there was lightness to his words, Sunainah also detected something deeper in his tone.

'And yet there is something else wrong, is there not?' She spoke softly and when she pulled up at a red light, she looked across at him. 'You do not have to tell me, Elliot. I am not the type of person to pry. It is nice that you and the children are here in Maroochydore, making a new life for yourselves. It is also good that you feel settled at the hospital. It is a fresh start, as you have said before.'

'One Marie's parents felt I was incapable of making.' The vehemence that accompanied his words did not surprise her because he had already mentioned that his wife's parents had tried to file for custody of his children. But why? What had given them cause to take such drastic action? It was clear to anyone who saw Elliot with Daphne and Joshua that he loved them. Before she could say anything, he shook his head.

'I'm sorry, Sunainah. I shouldn't drag you into the mess that is my life...or *was* my life.'

'I do not mind, Elliot. We are not only colleagues but I would also like to think we are friends so if you ever need someone to talk to, I am here to listen, if it is your wish.'

'Thank you, Sunainah.' He pushed his hand through his hair and nodded. They were friends. It was good to have women friends and the fact that he was constantly dreaming about this particular friend meant nothing, or so he was trying to tell himself. He felt that lately all he'd been doing had been pushing a very large burden uphill, trying to keep things in some sort of order so he didn't lose complete control of his life, but whenever he looked at Sunainah or saw her smile, or watched the graceful way she moved or listened to her soothing voice, he found himself drawn to her.

He was forever having to push the guilt away, the guilt that he was somehow cheating on Marie, that he was dishonouring her memory by moving on. The fact that Sunainah was willing to listen to what he had to say, was interested in what he had to say and was giving him her attention and support meant a great deal to him. He should at least tell her as much.

'That actually does help. Ever since we met, you've somehow managed to boost my confidence right when it's needed it the most.'

She smiled at his words. 'I am pleased but your confidence…did it really need the boost? You are an extremely competent doctor and it is clear after the week you have spent in the paediatric ward that you are excellent with the young patients—as you are with your own children.'

She shook her head, still confused. 'I do not see where your confidence would need any boosting.' The light turned green and she returned her attention to the road, more at ease now that there was actually a conversation taking place between them. That way, she could focus on what he was saying rather than the way his scent was teasing at her senses, driving her crazy.

'There you go again. Helping me out by telling me that I'm doing a good job. That's exactly what I'm talking about.'

'But I am merely speaking the truth.'

He nodded. 'That's because you are a nice person and it also makes it easier to accept what you're saying as the truth.'

'Why do you doubt yourself so much, Elliot?'

'Because others made me doubt.' His voice was soft and as she slowed the car and flicked on her indicator to turn into the doctors' car park at the hospital. Elliot continued to talk. 'When my wife died, it was as though my entire world had been ripped apart. I had an enormous gaping hole in my life, a fourteen-month-old little girl to somehow care for and a premature son fighting for his life. I didn't cope. I'm not ashamed to admit it because it's the truth. I fell to pieces.'

'It must have been incredibly stressful for you.' Sunainah understood the pain and anguish of loss and the fear and doubt that came along with it. She parked the car and turned off the engine but made no move to get out of the car. Neither did Elliot.

'Marie's parents were equally as devastated by her death. They'd been insistent that she terminate the pregnancy when she'd first been diagnosed, and when she had refused it had caused a big rift between them.' He shrugged one shoulder. 'I guess it was natural. As parents, they didn't want their daughter to die but Marie was stubborn.' His smile was small and intimate as he spoke of his wife.

Sunainah watched him closely, seeing the reflected happiness as he spoke of his wife. 'I am sure it could not have been an easy decision for the two of you to make.'

'No. It wasn't, but ultimately, as she'd pointed out to me several times, in the end it was *her* decision. She chose to put our son's life before her own.'

'Strong yet selfless.'

Elliot met her gaze, astonishment in his tone as he nodded. 'Exactly. That's exactly how she was. I knew you'd understand.'

Sunainah grimaced. 'I do.' She also understood, first-hand, the fallout from the difficult decisions other people made, but they were not talking about her. 'It would not have been easy for you to watch your wife go through so much pain and then afterwards to have little Joshua also fighting for his life.'

'No. That's why I turned to Marie's family, to her parents and sisters. I was spending every moment at the hospital, working in the unit, needing to bury myself and my grief in work as well as spend all of my free time by Joshua's side, hoping I wouldn't lose my son as well as my wife.'

'And Daphne?'

'She spent most of her time with her aunts and grand-parents.' He looked down at his hands for a moment before lifting his head and staring unwaveringly at Sunainah. 'The truth is I didn't want to face my life outside the hospital. Within those four walls I knew what was expected of me. I knew how to care for a sick, premature baby. I was trained to do that. I slept in the residential wing, ate my meals in the cafeteria and only saw Daphne when her aunts or grandparents brought her to the hospital.'

Sunainah's insides tightened at his words, at the way he had left his young daughter with grandparents— grandparents who had then tried to gain custody of their grandchildren. She closed her eyes, desperate to ignore the similarities with what had happened to her— but she had not been a young fourteen-month-old child. She had been a fourteen-year-old girl.

She swallowed over the dryness in her throat. Elliot did not need to hear about her horrible past and he did not need to dwell on matters that could not be changed. Instead, she said what he needed to hear. 'You were grieving for the loss of a loved one.'

'I was, but that's no excuse for abandoning my

daughter.' As he spoke the words his eyes became glazed with tears, and Sunainah immediately saw the similar expression her own father had worn when he had realised that *he*, too, had abandoned his daughter, leaving her in what he'd thought had been a safe environment. While he had been concentrating on her sick mother, wanting to spend every last moment with her, Sunainah had been fed to the lions.

'No. It is not.' She tried to keep her words calm and even but knew she had failed when Elliot's eyes widened a little in surprise. She looked away, unable to hold his gaze any longer. 'Daphne is young. She will not remember any of this.'

'True...but *I* will. Always.'

It was the same burden her father had carried, telling her he would deal with the situation, only...only he had let her down there as well. *Would* Elliot remember those sensations of having let Daphne down? Would he always protect his little girl? She knew she was probably being too hard on him, masking his situation with her own. She leaned over and placed a hand lightly on his.

'You are there for them now. This is what most matters.'

Elliot looked down at her hand, almost surprised by the touch. Immediately, Sunainah went to pull away, hoping he had not misconstrued her intention, but before she could do so he gave her fingers a little squeeze. 'You are a very giving and compassionate person, Sunainah Carrington.' He stared at her for a moment, his tone soft as though he was equally surprised at the natural chemistry that existed between them. 'We were definitely meant to meet.'

'I...I am sorry?' She shook her head a little, perplexed at the abrupt change of topic. 'I do not understand.'

'First I bump into you in the supermarket then discover I'll be working with you and that I live almost next door to you. It's fate.'

'No. It is hospital life.' Sunainah pulled her hand back, feeling her mind starting to slip into her dream world again as the tingles his touch had evoked continued to spread up her arm and burst like fireworks throughout her entire body. She needed to work harder at putting some distance between the two of them because there was no way any romantic relationship between them could end happily. She had tried romance five years ago with Raj. She had put her heart on the line and she had been rejected…and all because of her past. A past she was not responsible for but for which she still had to carry the burden.

'Hospital life?'

Sunainah sighed with a hint of exasperation as she unbuckled her seat belt. 'Mackenzie listed the town house on the hospital's accommodation website, which is specifically designed to assist new staff in securing a place to live close to the hospital.' She reached into the back of the car for her bag. 'The supermarket where we first met is the closest one to both the hospital and the cul-de-sac.' She opened the door and climbed from the car, Elliot following suit. 'We are both paediatricians so naturally we work in the same department. There is nothing to do with fate about any of that, just a lot of coincidence.'

Elliot closed the passenger door, his briefcase in his hand as he watched Sunainah lock the car and start

walking towards the hospital entrance. 'So you're saying you don't believe in fate but, rather, coincidence?'

'Fate is just someone else's way of trying to control
your life and no good ever came from doing that.'

'From doing what?' he queried, slightly confused.

'Controlling someone else's life.'

Elliot put out a hand to stop her and instead of walking off and causing a scene she stopped and looked politely at him. She had to ignore the way the concerned
look in his eyes pierced her heart.

He cared for her. Whether it was a friendship type
of caring or something else…something else she really
did not want to define, it was written there in his face.
She wanted to tell him not to. That it was not right for
any man to care for her, but the words would not leave
her throat.

All she was certain of right at this very instant was
that if she did not put some distance between herself
and Elliot, if she did not tell herself that all that existed
between them was nothing more than friendship, then
he would never discover the truth about her, about her
past, about what she had done. She could not bear for
him to look at her with contempt and disgust. She closed
her eyes for a moment.

'Sunainah?'

She opened her eyes but could not raise them to meet
his.

'What's wrong? Sunainah, what have I said that's
upset you?'

She shook her head and directed her words to the top
of his shirt collar. 'It is nothing, Elliot.' *I am nothing*,
she wanted to add, but knew if she did, there would be
far more questions coming from his lips.

Distance. It was imperative to get some distance between herself and Elliot, and with that she moved away from his touch, continuing towards the hospital.

It was nice of Elliot to show consideration for her feelings but she truly deserved no such attention from him. No, it was far better that from now on she keep her distance. They would be colleagues and neighbours. They would be polite to each other.

She could not let her past cause this good and caring man any more trouble. He was starting a new life, a life with his children. He would not have time for any romantic entanglements, and even if she had been a woman of good repute, a woman who had not been tainted by darkness and shame, he still would deserve someone better than her.

There was no way she could ever tell him of the growing feelings she was coming to have for him, feelings that were more than those of a friend or a colleague. These were feelings she had never truly experienced before, not this quickly or intensely. The problem was, her feelings for Elliot could definitely lead to deeper feelings and *they* would only bring about heartbreak for all concerned.

CHAPTER FIVE

ELLIOT WASN'T AT all sure what he'd done to annoy Sunainah and even though he tried to broach the subject with her a few times as they continued on their way to the ward, she really didn't seem in any mood to talk.

During the ward round, she appeared to be her usual self, calm, controlled and polite. Had he imagined the brief flash of pain that had pierced her features before she'd become Dr Brisk and Efficient? He watched as she smiled at William, her registrar; as she shared a joke with a patient; as she wrote up case notes after completing ward round; as she headed to the playroom to spend more time with the children.

He stood by the door to the playroom, pleased by the opportunity to watch her unawares for a few minutes as she sat in one of the small chairs, colouring with a little girl called Caitie, who had been admitted the previous day with a broken leg. The two were chatting, Caitie was giggling and Sunainah was her usual, graceful self.

Didn't she have any idea just how many knots she was tying him in? Ever since they'd met, he'd had a rotten time trying to remove her from his thoughts, especially after sneaking a small kiss to her cheek last week.

The soft smoothness of her skin had only given him

the thirst for more. Every time he'd seen her since, he'd breathed in her perfume, delighting in that summery scent. He'd admired the way she treated her patients and staff, how she listened to complaints and situations, weighing all the pros and cons before making the necessary decisions.

When he'd made the decision to move to Queensland, to change his Melbourne drizzle lifestyle for that of Maroochydore sunshine, the last thing he'd expected had been to meet a woman who refused to leave his thoughts.

During Marie's last few days, when the pain had been bad and there had been a great risk of the baby going into distress, she had made him promise that he would find someone new to share his life with, that he wouldn't be alone for the rest of his life.

'The kids will grow up and leave home one day, Elliot.' She had smiled wisely at him. 'Don't wait until then to find someone. Do it soon. She'll be someone special—just like me—and she'll love our kids with all her heart.'

Elliot had kissed Marie's lips to shut her up, not wanting to hear her talk so easily of another woman raising their children. Back then, he'd wanted to stop time, to press pause on their lives so he could take time to fully comprehend the enormous changes about to affect his life.

But now here he stood, watching as Sunainah sat at a small table, on a small chair, sharing small pencils with a small girl, both of them giggling together. She had a beautiful smile and a laugh that warmed his heart. When she spoke, he found her smooth, accented words relaxing.

Yes, he was attracted to her. Not only on a physical level but on an intellectual one as well. He wanted to talk to her about different topics, not just about medicine but about movies and books and politics and art and sport and absolutely every topic there was. He was intrigued by her, desperately wanting to know what had happened that morning to upset her.

He hadn't been looking for any type of romantic entanglement, preferring to focus his attention on his children and his job, determined to be the best paediatrician and father he could be. No, he definitely had not banked on meeting someone like Sunainah Carrington with her exotic beauty and charming mystique.

Caitie giggled and Sunainah laughed as well, the wonderful sound bringing him out of his reverie. When he refocused his attention on them, he realised both females were staring at him.

'Watchya doing?' Caitie asked as she giggled again. 'Dr Soo-nen-nah said you was holding up the wall. That's funny.'

Elliot grinned as he eased away from the wall, giving it a quick pat as though to reassure himself that it would not fall down without his strong presence before walking towards them. His actions only made Caitie giggle even more.

'May I join you, ladies?' Elliot asked as he pulled out one of the small chairs.

'Yes, yes, yes.' Caitie smiled brightly, holding out a pencil and handing him a sheet of paper. She was six years old and had been telling him earlier that she loved school and that when she grew up she was going to be a teacher. 'Dr Soo-nen-nah is doing a crazy picture.' Caitie giggled at the way Sunainah was choosing her colours. 'You're not supposed to colour the sky red and the trees purple.' She laughed as though it was the funniest thing she'd ever seen.

'It's good to be a little crazy sometimes.' Elliot admired Sunainah's picture when she held it up for his inspection. Sunainah didn't reply but she didn't scowl at him either. He took that as a good sign. Perhaps he'd imagined her mood earlier because now she was her usual amiable self, but when Nicole came to help Caitie with her crutches, saying it was time for her special bath, Sunainah started to pack up, not looking once in his direction.

'Wait, wait.' Caitie handed Sunainah the picture she'd coloured in. 'This is for you and I'll have the one you did.' Caitie looked at the strange colours on the picture and giggled again. 'It's so funny.'

Sunainah instantly accepted the little girl's drawing then levered herself up from the small chair and table. 'Thank you, Caitie. May I put your name and the date on this, then stick it up on the ward drawing board, please? Everyone must see your excellent skills.'

'Really?' Caitie's eyes were wide and filled with amazement. 'Really? On the wall? Like all the other pictures?'

'Yes. Absolutely.'

'Did you hear that, Nurse Nicole?'

Nicole took a moment to dutifully study the drawing. 'You're very clever, Caitie.' Nicole nodded then went back to shepherding Caitie from the playroom. Sunainah glanced quickly towards where Elliot still sat at the small table, once again unable to meet his gaze properly.

'I must go and finish my paperwork before there is

no sight of my desk.' She smiled politely in his direction and hot-footed it down the corridor.

'Beating a hasty retreat,' he murmured as he finished tidying up and setting the playroom to rights.

He realised that tidying things up had become second nature to him, knowing, as a single parent, that if he didn't do things, they would never get done. The realisation pleased him no end. He also realised that performing menial tasks gave him time to think, to ponder and consider, and as he worked he couldn't help but think of Sunainah, feeling perplexed at her behaviour.

They'd been talking about the way they'd met. He'd mentioned the word *fate* and she had completely changed. It had been an indication that perhaps there was a lot more to Sunainah Carrington than met the eye. It didn't matter whether or not she thought their meeting was fate, the fact of the matter was that they *had* met, and ever since they had he hadn't been able to get her off his mind.

Yes, the woman was absolutely stunning, especially with those expressive brown eyes of hers. Yes, she was a brilliant doctor with a wonderful and relaxed bedside manner. Yes, she had the most relaxing voice he'd ever heard, her dulcet tones helping to relax the tension in his shoulders. He'd had his doubts when Marie had been so sure he would meet someone else, and prior to his move to Maroochydore he hadn't even bothered thinking about dating.

He never would have believed that someone else's accent or the pitch of their voice could ever ease his tension in such a way, but he knew he could definitely listen to her talk about the most mundane and boring topics and yet still feel relaxed. It was a nice sensation, especially after the high-pitched nagging he'd endured during the past couple of years from his wife's family.

He exhaled slowly. Even *thinking* of the way Sunainah spoke filled him with a sense of calm that only made him more concerned that he'd inadvertently said something to upset her that morning.

Elliot walked towards the nurses' station, intent on doing some of his own paperwork, but after he'd sat reading the same sentence three times over he couldn't shake the feeling that he needed to talk to her. It wasn't like Sunainah to be so stilted and polite. True, he'd only known her for just over a week but they'd already shared so much, from cleaning up after sick children to sharing dinner with friends. Even Daphne had been asking to see Soo-*nen*-nah again and last night Joshua had joined in with the chorus. 'Nen-nah,' he'd added to his sister's chant.

Elliot had laughed and told both his children they'd see Sunainah soon enough, but now he had the feeling that might not be the case. He recalled the way she hadn't been able to meet his gaze, the way she'd been a little jumpy when he'd come into the playroom, and how the instant Nicole had come to whisk Caitie away Sunainah had also high-tailed it out of there, as though she hadn't wanted to be left alone with him.

He closed the case notes with such force he made the nurse seated beside him jump.

'Something wrong, Elliot?' she asked.

'Er...no.' He thought quickly for a moment. He needed to talk to Sunainah. It was best he find out what he'd done to upset her and apologise immediately. The last thing he wanted was for her to feel uncomfortable at work, in her own department, simply because he'd been an insensitive cad, even if he hadn't realised it.

'Actually, yes. Yes, there is something wrong.' He picked up the case notes and tucked them under his arm. 'I think I need to discuss this patient with Sunainah.' As a cover, it was one good one. Doctors were always discussing their patients with other doctors.

The nurse nodded. 'Nothing *I* can help with?' There was an interested gleam in her eyes and he didn't miss the double entendre of her words. Elliot smiled nervously but shook his head.

'I think it's Sunainah I need.' Without another word he turned on his heel and headed down the corridor towards Sunainah's office. He glanced back over his shoulder, noticing the nurse was watching him carefully, a look of delight on her face, as though he were a cream pie and she wanted to eat him.

Feeling rather awkward, Elliot knocked twice on Sunainah's office door then, wanting to escape the leering nurse's gaze, he opened the door and entered the office without waiting for Sunainah's permission.

His thoughts quickly turned from the nurse to the woman before him who, much to his surprise and astonishment, was sitting behind her desk, tissues in hand, sobbing quietly.

'Sunainah?'

'Uh…Elliot!' She stared at him for a whole second, one that seemed to last far longer, before quickly composing herself, blowing her nose and sitting up straighter in her chair. 'My apologies.' She cleared her throat and forced a polite smile. 'What can I help you with?'

Elliot immediately walked towards her, putting the

case notes on the desk before coming around to kneel by her chair.

'I think it's me who can help you. What's wrong?'

'Oh? Uh...' She shook her head. 'Sometimes I just need an outlet. To cry.'

'Are you worried about Caitie?'

'No. No. She is doing a tremendous job of getting better.' She dabbed once at her eyes then put the tissue into the bin before starting to straighten the papers on her desk. 'Sometimes, although I am happy to see them get better and head home, I do worry. And I miss them. Like Rory and Matthew and Dean. They're all now coping at home and although I will see them in my clinic in a few weeks' time, sometimes the leaving part can make me quite sad.'

Elliot nodded, watching her closely for a few moments, noticing the way she still wasn't meeting his gaze. His gut instinct told him there was far more going on here than she was saying. 'Are you sure that's all that's upsetting you?'

'Of course. Releasing the tension. All doctors do it.'

He watched her for another moment then decided that if she didn't want to talk to him, she didn't have to. Perhaps whatever was on her mind was too new, too scary, too intense to discuss openly. If that was the case, he was right there with her. This natural attraction between them was something he was butting heads with on a daily basis. If, by some crazy random happenstance, Sunainah felt the same way, then he most definitely understood her confusion.

He nodded again then stood, realising it was probably better to change the subject. 'That's good. It's good you know when to release the tension. I release my tension by cooking.'

'Cooking?' That did surprise her and she immediately met his gaze. It was a mistake. To look into those wonderful blue eyes…eyes that seemed to have the ability to see right down into her very soul… She looked away before he saw anything too private and went back to organising her desk.

'Yes. In fact, why don't you come round for dinner this evening?'

Her hands stilled for a moment but she managed to resist the temptation to look at him. 'Thank you for the invitation, Elliot, but as you can see from the state of my desk I must get this paperwork under control this evening.'

'Bring it along.' He strode round to the other side of her desk, picking up the case notes he'd entered with. 'Once Daphne and Joshua are in bed, we can sit down and tackle those papers together. You'll get through it a lot quicker and it will also help me to learn the department's protocols a bit better.'

'Uh…' She watched as he headed to the door, smiling warmly at her over his shoulder, exuding that natural charm of his that made it difficult for her to resist him. It was right that she should distance herself from him and the children, that she should refuse his kind offer, but the words somehow did not seem to come to her lips.

'Both Daphne and Joshua have been asking to see you again, to spend some time with you. Plus, it's Joshie's second birthday next weekend and I was hoping you'd be able to help me with the planning.' He looked down at his feet for a moment then met her eyes once more. 'I'm afraid I didn't do much last year to celebrate his first birthday so I'd like to make it up to him this year.'

She was silent, staring at him with a mixture of delight and regret.

'Help me, please? For Joshie?' he added, knowing his words were bordering on emotional blackmail but right now all he could think about was getting her to agree. Whatever was bothering her was clearly something she couldn't discuss at work. Being at home, in a relaxed environment, was a much better way to entice her to open up more to him.

'It would be nice for him to have a party but—'

'Excellent. I'll see you tonight. Around six would be great.' With that, he winked at her and headed out of her office before she could decline.

Sunainah continued to sit, staring at her closed door. How had that happened? Not three hours ago she had been lecturing herself to be nothing more than a professional colleague and a polite neighbour towards Elliot, and now, somehow, she was going round to his place for dinner to not only spend time with him and his children and help plan Joshua's birthday party but also to focus on work. Was there any part of her life this man had not somehow managed to infiltrate?

The phone on her desk rang and she immediately picked it up, pleased with the interruption.

'Hey, there.' Mackenzie's voice came down the line.

'Er…hello.'

'I've just spoken to Reggie and Bergan. We've all got forty-five minutes spare to head across the road to the café for a quick lunch. Any chance you're free in about half an hour?'

Sunainah looked at her paperwork then closed her

eyes. With Elliot's promise to help her tonight, she would be able to get things sorted. Plus, she could really use the diversion of seeing her friends. That way she could forget about Elliot Jones and her upcoming evening.

'Sounds perfect,' she replied with relief. 'See you then.' Sunainah hung up the phone and stared at the work on her desk. She closed her eyes, unable to think about anything except the way Elliot had burst into her office and found her crying.

She was extremely grateful he had not pushed the subject, because if he had, he would have realised she had been crying because of him, because of the way he made her feel and how she simply seemed unable to control the overwhelming need for him to hold her close.

Just once. She wanted to feel what it was like to have his arms around her. She raised a hand to her cheek where his lips had left an invisible mark on her skin and wished she had had the courage to return the favour. She had often dreamed of him kissing her, of smiling down at her as he declared his attraction to her.

'But it is just a dream,' she told herself, snapping her thoughts back to reality. 'And you need to get at least *some* work done before meeting your friends for lunch.' To that end, she straightened her shoulders and took the first piece of paper from her in-tray.

Later, as she walked through the hospital with Mackenzie, heading across the road to the coffee shop, she at least felt a small sense of accomplishment, having dealt with at least three small things in that half-hour. Perhaps she wouldn't need to spend too long at Elliot's tonight, working side by side with him. She shook the thought away as her stomach started to churn with anticipated delight.

'I hear you have a dinner date with Elliot,' Mackenzie said as they walked along.

Sunainah almost tripped. She stared at her friend in mortification. 'How did you hear that?' Was there already hospital gossip about this impromptu dinner?

Mackenzie laughed at the look on her friend's face. 'Don't stress it. I bumped into Elliot just now in the stairwell. I invited him and the children to join us for dinner tonight as John has the day off and will be doing all the cooking. So imagine my surprise when he tells me he's unavailable as he already has plans tonight—with you.'

'It is business, Mackenzie. He is helping me with the paperwork and learning more about the department.'

'And in return you'll help him plan Joshie's second birthday party.' Mackenzie waggled her eyebrows up and down then clapped her hands with glee. 'It's good, Sunainah. This is a good development. He is definitely into you.'

'What? No, he is not.'

Mackenzie stared at her as though she was thick. 'What man in his right mind offers to help a woman as beautiful as you with just paperwork?'

Sunainah stopped in the middle of the road and stared at her friend in complete astonishment. 'Do you mean he will not help me?'

Mackenzie laughed and grabbed Sunainah's arm, pulling her to the other side of the road. 'I'm saying that Elliot is interested in you. Seriously, Sunainah.'

'No. You are wrong. He is still in love with his wife.'

'He might have moved on,' Mackenzie suggested.

Sunainah shook her head again. 'He cannot be interested in me and if he does not help me with my work tonight then I must go back to my office right now and at least get something done.'

'Of course he'll help you.' Mackenzie rolled her eyes. 'He's the type of man to help a damsel in distress.'

'I am not in distress. Just busy.'

The two of them walked into the café where Reggie and Bergan were waiting for them. Sunainah immediately turned to Mackenzie, a pleading tone in her words. 'Please do not discuss this with the others. Not yet. I am sure you are wrong about Elliot. You have to be because I am not the woman for him. In fact, I am not the woman for any man. Please, I do not want a post-mortem of my life, past, present or speculative future, over lunch.'

'All right. If you insist, but we will be discussing this at a future date. Mark it in your diary, my darling Sunainah. And where your past is concerned, perhaps it's now time to deal with it.'

Sunainah instantly shook her head but Mackenzie nodded, her tone encouraging.

'You *can* deal with it. You're much stronger than you realise but I also want you to tell me exactly why you think you are not right for our new handsome neighbour because I think you're made for each other.'

Were they? Made for each other? Sunainah shook her head, clearing her thoughts as she focused on enjoying the company of her friends, but all throughout the lunch and indeed throughout the rest of the day she kept wondering why Mackenzie thought she might be a good match for Elliot.

* * *

'Daddy. Phone. Daddy. Phone.' Daphne was calling louder than the ringing phone as Elliot finished stirring the pasta sauce in preparation for his dinner with Sunainah.

'All right, all right. I'm answering it,' he said as he connected the call, smiling at his daughter, who was busy playing with her toys, trying to keep her favourite doll out of Joshua's reach. 'Hello?'

'Elliot?'

'Gillian?' The last person he had expected to hear from tonight was his sister-in-law.

'Have I caught you at a bad time?'

'No. It's all right. I just…hadn't expected to hear from you.'

'You mean after the appalling way my family treated you?'

'Well, there is that.' Elliot started layering the pasta sauce and lasagne sheets into the dish as he waited for Gillian to reveal the purpose of her call.

'So…how are you?'

'Good.'

'And the children?'

'They're both fine. Joshua had a bit of a cold but he's all right now.'

'Poor baby.'

'What about you? How's Linus? The kids?'

'They're all well. Linus is still at work but should be home soon.' There was a pause, and Elliot was determined not to fill it. Out of all of Marie's family Gillian was the only he was willing to maintain contact with. It had been Gillian who had alerted him to the fact that Marie's parents had been intent on filing for custody of Daphne and Joshua and it had been Gillian who had apologised to him for her terrible behaviour.

'I was grieving the loss of my sister,' she'd told him not long before he'd made the decision to leave Melbourne. 'I took it out on you. I'm sorry, Elliot.'

When she didn't speak, he decided to push for the reason. 'So, Gillian, what can I help you with?'

'Nothing really. I was just thinking that Joshua's birthday is coming up and wondered if you were planning on having a party or…something.'

'Yes we are having a party. In fact, a friend is coming around tonight to help me.' He finished layering the lasagne and put it in the oven to bake.

'A…female friend?'

'She's my neighbour.'

'Oh, really?' He could tell Gillian was smiling as she absorbed this information. 'Well, that's great, Elliot. I'm happy for you.'

'She's just a friend, Gill.' But even as he said the words he knew it wasn't exactly true. Sunainah was… He closed his eyes for a moment as he tried to figure it out. She was his neighbour, his colleague and his friend. Of that he was certain, but she had to be more than a friend given he couldn't seem to stop dreaming or thinking about her.

'Marie told me she wanted you to find someone else. She wanted you to be happy, Elliot. You do know that, don't you?'

It was odd. He'd had these same discussions with himself but hearing Gillian's voice on the phone, sounding so much like Marie's, Elliot felt the love he still had for his wife fill his heart. But it wasn't the same as before. It was a love tinged with sadness and regret.

'She told me. Only hours before she died she told me to find someone else.' He shook his head as he leaned against the bench. He opened his eyes and looked off into the past, seeing Marie lying in the stark white hospital bed, Joshua's humidi-crib as close as he could get it. 'I vowed after her death never to move on. That it would never happen.'

'But this woman? Your friend who's coming over tonight…she would have to be someone special, right? I mean, if she's going to replace Marie—'

'No one will ever replace Marie,' he interrupted.

'Of course not,' Gillian instantly agreed. 'Bad choice of words. All I meant was that this woman, if she's even made you think of moving forward, must be someone special. Really special.'

Elliot closed his eyes, easily picturing Sunainah's face. Her twinkling eyes, her white teeth, her exotic scent, her jet-black hair he was almost itching to free from the pins she bound it with. Yes, she was someone special and she was starting to drive him to distraction.

'Yes.' His voice was soft. 'Yes, Gillian, she is someone special.'

'Good to hear.' Gillian sighed long and loud. 'I have to say I'm relieved.'

'You are?'

'Yes.'

'Why?'

'Because Marie made me promise to help you to move on eventually. I've done a pretty lousy job of it so far but now, hearing you so happy, knowing the kids are settling in…it's all good news, Elliot.'

'It's scary, Gill.'

Gillian laughed. 'Of course it is.'

'What if this…friend turns out to be nothing more than a friend? What if I'm making a huge mistake? What if I do more damage to my children by introducing them to a woman who has absolutely no interest in me?' It wasn't until he finished speaking that he even realised his confusion had run that deep.

'You're a smart man, Elliot. You took a chance on Marie and you were both very happy.'

'True.' Elliot walked to the archway to watch his children playing together. He'd already made so many mistakes during their short lives and although they wouldn't remember them, he always would. Was Sunainah someone who would stick around? Become part of their family? She liked his children, of that he was certain. He was fairly sure she liked him, too, even though she often gave him mixed signals.

'Take a chance, eh?'

'Living life is good,' Gillian replied, and after she'd rung off and Elliot had finished preparing the salad, he realised the chances he'd taken recently really had paid off. Sure, he'd uprooted his family but he'd found a better job at a nicer hospital with great staff. He was a member of the cul-de-sac crew, had found a brilliant daycare centre for his children and had wonderful neighbours.

Things were definitely starting to look up for him and perhaps it was time to take a bigger chance…to see exactly where these strange but exciting emotions he felt for Sunainah took him.

That night, Sunainah looked at herself critically in the mirror, wondering what her friends saw that she did not. She was a woman with a dark complexion, dark eyes and dark hair. She was nothing special. Tonight she had dressed in a pair of three-quarter denim jeans and a loose-fitting cotton shirt that was almost like a dress it was so long. She had released her hair from its usual bun and plaited it in one long plait that hung halfway down her back. She had thought about leaving it loose before she'd remembered that this was technically a business dinner so she should at least look tidy, rather than having hair everywhere.

At the appointed time she headed to Elliot's town house, carrying a big bottle of fruit squash and sparkling mineral water as an offering to her host. Her paperwork was in a bag slung over her shoulder. 'This is business. This is business,' she repeated to herself as she rang the front door bell.

'Come on in, Sunainah,' she heard Elliot call, and no sooner had she stepped inside than there was the patter of tiny footsteps heading in her direction.

'Soo-*nen*-nah!' Daphne called.

'Nen-nah!' Joshua joined in.

Sunainah quickly put her shoulder bag by the door, holding firmly to the drinks as two little people, filled with excited delight, wrapped their chubby arms about her legs.

'Nen-nah. Nen-nah,' Joshua repeated over and over again.

'Pick me up. Pick me up.' Daphne let go of Sunainah's leg but started jumping up and down beside her, her little arms outstretched pleadingly.

'Me, too. Me, too,' Joshua replied, following his big sister's actions.

Sunainah laughed, leaning over to put the drinks onto a nearby table before scooping first Daphne then

Joshua into her arms. She hugged them tight, laughing at their infectious exuberance. As she straightened up, one child on each hip, she glanced over to the kitchen doorway, where she saw Elliot, tea towel over his shoulder, leaning against the archway, a wide grin on his face.

'I see you have been successfully welcomed,' he remarked, and when he noticed the bottles of drink on the table he walked over and picked them up, a quizzical look on his face as though he had no idea how they'd got there.

'A token contribution towards our meal. I was not sure what we would be eating and, besides, I did not want the children to feel left out so I brought something we could all drink.'

Elliot looked from the drinks back to her, the woman holding his two children, the children who had their arms wrapped tightly about her neck, big smiles on their faces. He ignored a pang of jealousy, wanting to do exactly the same thing. Never had he thought he'd be jealous of his own children! 'You're very thoughtful, Sunainah, and clearly understand children.'

'It is my job.'

'No.' Elliot shook his head and took a few steps closer towards her. 'Your job,' he continued, his voice quiet, 'is to provide medical care for your patients. Everything else you do, the way you relate to the children on their own level, doing jigsaws, colouring in or keeping a necklace made from macaroni is what clearly shows just how much you truly care.'

He came closer still, into her own personal space, and for a moment Sunainah had no clue what to do. Daphne and Joshua were still holding tightly to her neck, resting their little heads on her shoulders. She could not step back to put some much-needed distance between herself and Elliot because she did not want to accidentally trip over one of the kids' toys that might be on the floor. Instead, she lifted her chin a little, trying to show that she was not at all uncomfortable with his close proximity.

'You're a good doctor, a good friend and a really nice person, Sunainah.' His tone dropped lower. 'I like that about you. *Really* like that about you.' He let the words hang in the air for a moment before his gaze dipped from her eyes to take in the contours of her mouth.

Sunainah swallowed, her heart pounding wildly against her chest as she tried hard to concentrate on what she was supposed to be doing. How could he say words like that and look at her with such intensity that it truly made her mind go completely blank? If someone had asked for her name, she would not have been able to tell them, such was the effect Elliot had on her cognitive functions.

'Er...' Her lips parted to release the sound and she watched as Elliot's gaze dipped to stare at her mouth, taking in the small action. The spicy scent she equated with him wound its way about her senses, helping to keep her focus solely on him and how he was making her feel.

It was wrong for her to feel this way. To feel happiness and excitement and confusion and uncertainty simply because Elliot did not seem to be able to stop staring at her mouth...and, much to her surprise, and embarrassment, she belatedly realised, she was staring back at him.

What did it mean? Had Mackenzie been right? Did Elliot find her attractive? His words had implied as much but she had been fed romantic lines before that had turned out to be nothing more than a farce.

'Daddy, Daddy, Daddy.' Joshua's little voice pierced the fog surrounding the adults as he lifted his head from Sunainah's shoulder and held out his hands towards his father. Elliot shook his head, as though to clear it, and immediately put the drinks down and took his son from Sunainah's arms. Daphne was more than delighted with having Sunainah all to herself but gave her father a pleading look.

'I'm hungry, Daddy.'

'Yes. Yes. Of course.' Elliot shifted Joshua to one hip and then picked up the bottle of squash, carrying it into the kitchen, glad of the very small respite from Sunainah's enchanting presence. What was it about this woman that was making him act like a hormonal teen-ager? He'd practically been leaning in to plant a kiss on her lips while she'd been holding his children. Where was his self-control?

It wasn't the first time he'd wanted to kiss her and if he was honest with himself right now it wouldn't be the last, but as he'd looked at her he couldn't help but no-tice the concern and worry evident in her eyes. Didn't she want his attentions? Had he read the signals wrong? He was certain she felt that same irrepressible tug, that same awareness, that same need that had started to burn through him almost from the first moment they'd met.

She was exotic, unique and different from any other woman he'd ever known. Perhaps that was his indication that if anything on a deeply personal level was going to happen between himself and Sunainah, he needed to proceed with care.

As she followed him into the kitchen, Daphne securely in her arms and the bottle of mineral water in hand, he turned and looked at her, his gut tightening at her stunning beauty.

Proceed with care. Proceed with care.

The words kept repeating on a loop inside his head and he knew he needed to heed their warning because he had the deep and abiding sensation that Sunainah was not only worthy of his slow and careful attention but also she deserved to be treated as though she was the most precious woman in the world.

CHAPTER SIX

ELLIOT WAS JEALOUS of his children and the ease with which they hugged and kissed Sunainah. She reciprocated, cuddling them and making them laugh. Over dinner, she'd asked both children what they would like to do to celebrate Joshua's birthday.

Elliot sat back in his chair and watched—it never had occurred to him to actually *ask* the children. Joshie was only turning two. How could he possibly know what he wanted? Yet by the end of dinner, all of them enjoying the home-made lasagne with crusty bread and salad, it was decided they would spend Joshua's birthday at the beach, having a barbecue, making sandcastles and splashing in the water.

Afterwards, while Elliot insisted on clearing up, Sunainah sat on the floor with his children, Daphne fetching cushions for them all, and taught them some cute games with hand claps and singing, challenging the children's fine motor skills. His daughter surprised him further when she presented Sunainah with a long necklace made from buttons.

'Did you make this for me?' Sunainah's eyes were wide with delighted happiness as she put the long chain over her head as Daphne nodded enthusiastically.

'At Grandma Liz's,' she told Sunainah proudly.

'I *love* it.' Sunainah placed her hand over her chest, over the necklace, her words filled with emotion. Daphne hugged and kissed Sunainah several times, her little face alive with a delight Elliot had never seen before.

Joshua crawled onto Sunainah's lap, generally made himself at home, snuggling into her as though it was the one place in the world he was assured of complete security. It was clear that the children loved her.

'I think he's getting tired,' Sunainah said ten minutes later. 'He is starting to get heavier.'

'His eyes are starting to droop,' Elliot confirmed, rising from the floor. 'Ouch.' He laughed as his knee cracked.

'Getting old?' Sunainah couldn't help but smile at his antics of putting his hands on his lower back and stretching his cramped muscles.

The smile quickly slid from her face as she watched him surreptitiously. The way the hem of his cotton shirt rose up, the way his khaki shorts dipped, revealing a strip of perfectly firm abdominal muscles. Sunainah tried her hardest not to stare. She was a doctor, for goodness' sake. It wasn't as though she hadn't seen a man's abdominal muscles before, but Elliot was not a patient and she could not look upon him in an objective, impartial light.

Her insides tightened, her mouth went dry and her body zinged to life in a way she had never experienced in her entire life. Elliot had a good body. A good, firm, hard, solid, manly, muscular—

'Sunainah?' His voice was a soft caress, one that held the slightest hint of male pride. She immediately raised her gaze to meet his and felt her cheeks suffuse with heat at the small, satisfied smirk on his lips and one slightly raised eyebrow.

'Y-yes?' She closed her eyes for a moment, unable to believe her voice had completely failed her. Clearing her throat, she looked just below his chin, focusing on his throat, but even that was bad enough. The smooth skin revealed beneath his open-necked shirt was almost as tantalising as the rest of his gorgeous body.

She had never been the type of woman to judge anyone on their looks, let alone a man who was her colleague, but she could not deny the way the slightest glimpse of Elliot's body had effectively caused her feminine need to zoom into overdrive. It was most improper but at this moment she could not give a thought to propriety. She needed to regroup, to control her wayward emotions, to focus on getting out of his house as soon as possible without appearing rude.

'Here. Let me take Joshua from you.' Elliot leaned forward and Sunainah instantly held her breath, not wanting to acknowledge the comforting warmth emanating from him or the glorious way he smelled. His hand brushed her arm and she couldn't stop the audible gasp that left her lips, her eyes widening with surprise. This man was affecting her way too much.

With his son removed from her lap, Sunainah instantly stood, taking great care to brush a hand down her shirt and jeans and adjust her beautiful necklace, giving them attention they did not require. She was not at all sure what to say or to do next. What did a woman say to a man when he had caught her staring at him as though she wanted nothing more than to cover his body with kisses? Thankfully, little Daphne came to her rescue.

'Soo-*nen*-nah. Soo-*nen*-nah!' Daphne held out her arms towards her, and Sunainah instantly obliged, hugging the child close as though needing her as a shield.

Elliot's small smile indicated he knew exactly what she was doing and she realised that whatever had previously existed between her new colleague and herself had dramatically changed within the past minute. How on earth was she supposed to bring the world around her back into alignment?

'Would…?' She stopped and swallowed again, clearing her throat once more, determined her voice would sound calm and controlled. 'Would you like me to get Daphne settled while you organise Joshua?' She still could not completely meet his gaze but instead focused on the small boy resting happily in his father's arms.

That was another mistake because man and boy— together—looked wonderful. Good heavens. Two perfect specimens of the male sex. And not only that, the way Elliot clearly loved his son was evident in the way those big, strong arms held the child securely, as if to say he would protect and love him for ever. The sight warmed her heart and she hugged little Daphne closer, wanting to promise the same thing to her.

'Thank you, Sunainah. That would be helpful.' That satisfied grin was still on his lips but she did her best to ignore it, not wanting to delve into what it might mean. 'Daphne knows her night-time routine.'

'Yes, I remember.'

'Of course. You put her to bed last week, so the two of you should be fine.' He looked at his daughter.

'Daddy will be up soon to read you a story and give you goodnight cuddles.'

'Okey-dokey,' Daphne replied, making both adults chuckle, the sound doing much to settle Sunainah's pounding heart. With that, she carried Daphne upstairs, eager for a bit of space between the two of them, while Elliot took his sleeping son to the downstairs bedroom. She followed all Daphne's instructions again and in record time the little girl was in her nightie and snuggled into the bed, which looked way too large for her.

'What do we do now?' Sunainah asked her.

'Daddy reads stories but you sing. Sing now, Soo-*nen*-nah. Sing.'

'Manners?' Sunainah raised her eyebrows and Daphne immediately looked contrite.

'Please, sing, Soo-*nen*-nah?'

'Nice manners,' she praised. 'What song would you like me to sing? A nursery rhyme?'

Daphne shook her head. 'That song. *That* song.' Then, when Sunainah continued to frown at her, Daphne tried to say some of the foreign words.

'Oh.' Realisation dawned on Sunainah. 'The Indian lullaby?'

'Yes.' Daphne patted the side of her bed. 'Ind-an lull-a-ly. Lie down.'

'Manners?' Sunainah prompted again.

'Lie down, please?' Daphne corrected herself. She shifted over in the bed to make room for Sunainah, who did as she had been bidden and was delighted when Daphne snuggled into her. Slowly, Sunainah began to sing the lullaby her mother had often sung to her as a little girl, a lullaby that had always made her feel safe and secure, and as she sang it to Daphne, she hoped to evoke the same sensations.

It was the same song she had sung to herself as a hurt and dejected fourteen-year-old, so alone in such a foreign place. She would curl into a small ball in her bed, singing it almost in a whisper so as not to awaken—

Sunainah cut the thought off and looked at the little girl beside her, only then realising Daphne's breathing was measured and calm, indicating she was most likely sound asleep. Sunainah tried to shift, to see whether the little girl's eyes were open or closed.

'She's out of it.' Elliot's smooth voice spoke quietly from the doorway. 'That song really is beautiful or perhaps it's just the way you sing it.' He came farther into the room as Sunainah carefully extracted herself from Daphne's hold without waking the child.

'Joshua?' she asked.

'The same as his sister,' Elliot whispered as he walked over and brushed a loving hand over Daphne's forehead, pushing the hair from her face. He bent and kissed his daughter before turning to face Sunainah. 'You have no idea just how much pressure you've taken off me simply by putting her to bed. Thank you.' With Daphne sleeping soundly, her fairy-princess night-light providing the room with a comforting amber glow, he indicated they should leave the room. 'After you.'

Sunainah nodded and headed down the stairs.

'Ready to get some work done?' He spoke in his normal voice. 'That was the deal after all.'

Sunainah looked at the bag she had left by the door and shook her head. 'It is later than I anticipated and I will be more than able to get things organised. We do not need to worry about—' But even as she spoke Elliot had crossed to the door and retrieved the bag, carrying it to the large dining-room table.

'A deal is a deal and it's only just gone eight o'clock. That's not late at all and you know it.'

It would be easier for her to yield rather than argue, so Sunainah sat down at the table, pleased when he seemed to slip into professional mode. She was concerned he would mention the way she had ogled him earlier, the way she could not think straight when he stared deeply into her eyes or when he winked at her.

Sometimes he would look at her as though he could not wait to press his lips firmly to hers and hold her as close as possible, their bodies firm against each other. She wanted to deny the yearning for his firm, strong arms to be around her, feeling the security they would provide, a security she desperately craved. She did not need him to take over her life but instead to support her, to let her know she was special, that she was worthy of receiving such emotions from another person.

Instead, he politely offered her a hot drink then set to work. By the time it was half past nine they had made definite progress through the majority of the papers she had brought with her.

'So you just need to check these three files with Bethany tomorrow, wait for reports on these two patients and everything is then shipshape and in order,' he remarked, leaning back in his chair and stretching his arms above his head. This time Sunainah forced herself to look away, not wanting to be caught once again ogling her colleague.

'Thank you so much, Elliot. It is very clear you have experience in running a busy department.' She started gathering the papers together, needing to put them back into the bag and get out of his house as soon as possible. His scent was becoming far too intoxicating and now, without the children providing a natural distraction, it was imperative for her to put as much distance between them as possible.

'I really do appreciate your assistance.' She could not even look his way, unsure whether or not he was still stretching. The sight of his body earlier had been enough to inflame a need she had not even realised she had. The best way to resist temptation was to remove the temptation.

Even now, she knew once she was alone in her home she would have difficulty controlling her thoughts, unable to avoid reflecting on the wonderful evening she had enjoyed, both with him and his children. Why did he have to be so…fantastic? They had laughed, played and worked hard. She connected with him on so many levels and that was definitely a problem because it made him hard to ignore.

Sunainah stood, making sure her bag was securely closed so nothing fell out. She could still not bring herself to look Elliot's way, so when his voice came from right beside her, she jumped.

'Are you all right?' His words were quiet with an intimate feel to them.

She tried to edge back a little. 'Yes. I am fine.' She glanced once in his direction before picking up her bag and forcing herself to walk away. Distance was imperative. 'I have really appreciated the amount of paperwork we have managed to—'

'You've already said that,' he interrupted. 'You don't need to rush off, Sunainah. Would you like a glass of wine?' He spread his hands wide. 'Or perhaps a cup of tea? I think I have chai.'

'I am not big on tea drinking.' At his raised eyebrows she nodded, unable to stop a small smile from touching the corners of her lips. 'I know. You would think that having an Indian mother and an English father I would be a connoisseur of tea drinking but…no. I much prefer coffee.'

'Good to know.' He nodded as though he was filing the information away for future reference. 'At any rate, there's no reason to rush off.' He couldn't stop his need to prolong her visit. Ever since she'd arrived, they had been busy doing something, eating or playing with the children or working, and now all he wanted was to sit and chat with her, to get to know her better. And if one thing led to another and he ended up kissing her, then that was completely fine with him.

'I think there is. No doubt your children will be up with the birds so you also need to sleep.'

'Sunainah, you seem rather anxious to leave. Is anything wrong?' Elliot took a step closer. 'Have I done or said something to offend you?'

'Er…no.' She took a step back, almost bumping into a packing box. She quickly sidestepped the box, needing to keep as much distance between herself and Elliot as possible. 'I am fine but I do thank you for your concern.'

'Oh, I am concerned about you, Sunainah. Very concerned.'

'You are?' Surprised, she stopped by the front door, one hand on the handle, the other holding the bag. He came closer and closer and she simply stood there, waiting, watching, wanting. Her heart hammered against her ribs and her knees started to wobble as his glorious scent flooded her senses. She could not move, feeling like a deer trapped in the headlights of an oncoming car.

He made no move to touch her but when he spoke his words were like silk, winding around them, binding them together.

'Can't you feel it?' His tone had dropped, his words powerful and intimate.

'I am not sure I under—'

Elliot pressed his finger softly to her lips. At the contact, Sunainah gasped. Her mind went blank. Her vocal cords refused to function. Her legs were not receiving the signals from her brain that told them to flee.

He stepped even closer, breaching her personal space, and yet she immediately wanted him even closer. She stood there, hands itching to touch him, to grab his shirt and haul him up against her. Good heavens. How was it possible he could affect her in such a way?

'Can you feel it…now?' he whispered, lowering his hand. He made no other effort to touch her. Instead, he just looked, drinking his fill of her perfect skin, her rosy cheeks, her wide eyes and her perfectly formed mouth. 'Do you know, I often find myself daydreaming about what you would look like with your hair flowing loose about your shoulders? Even in this plait it looks so glossy and soft.' He edged even closer to her, and she swallowed nervously.

'I would like nothing better now than to release it from its bonds and run my hands through it, to feel the silky texture as it slips through my fingers.' He exhaled slowly, his gaze flicking between her parted lips and surprised eyes.

'Does that bother you? That I want to touch your

hair? That I want to hold you close? That I can't stop dreaming about you?'

'D-dreaming?'

'Yes. During the day, when I'm supposed to be concentrating on work. Dreaming about you at night, when I'm supposed to be concentrating on… Well, I'm not supposed to be concentrating at all but the point is, you appear to be on my mind more often than not, Sunainah.'

'I am…sorry.' She closed her eyes, unable to believe he was saying such wonderful words to her. Her breathing had increased and she parted her lips to allow the pent-up air to escape. They both knew she could leave at any time. He was not holding her captive. All she needed to do was to turn the door handle and she would be able to walk out of his home and escape into the darkness of the night.

She didn't. The truth was, she *wanted* to stand right where she was, close to him, listening to him saying such wonderful words to her. Never had any man made her feel the way Elliot was making her feel right now. Yet…she was not worthy of a man like Elliot and it would be wrong to lead him on.

'Sunainah? Have I…shocked you?' There was a hint of doubt in his words and it was enough to make her look at him again.

'No man has ever said such beautiful words to me before.'

Elliot raked an unsteady hand through his hair. 'I find that hard to believe.'

'And yet I speak the truth.' She smiled at him. 'Elliot, I thank you for giving me this honour.'

'But…?' he prompted.

'I do not think we should pursue anything other than a friendship.'

A frown immediately creased his brow. 'Why?'

'Why? Why does there need to be a reason?'

'Is there someone else?'

'No.'

'Was there ever anyone else? I mean, do you often date? Have you been engaged?' He pushed a hand through his hair. 'There is still so much I don't know about you and I want to, Sunainah. I really want to.'

She shook her head slowly from side to side. 'Elliot. I cannot—'

'Have you ever been engaged? Just answer, yes or no.'

She sighed and tried not to think of just how close his mouth was to her, of how it would take next to nothing for her to ease up and press a kiss to his lips. He was truly driving her to distraction but perhaps if she told him a bit about her past, he would understand *why* she was trying to spare both of them much pain and heartache by ending things before they had the opportunity to begin.

'I was engaged. Five years ago.'

'What happened?'

'He changed his mind.' She shrugged a shoulder. 'One minute I was preparing for a wedding and the next he was leaving town, breaking up with me via a text message.'

Elliot shook his head in disgust. 'What a fool.'

'I do not know about that but it turned out to be best for both of us. Besides, I have work to focus on. I do not have time for romantic entanglements.' She touched the button necklace as she spoke, needing to keep her fingers busy so she did not reach out and touch Elliot, as she so desperately wanted to do.

'Oh. Well, that's good.' He chuckled, and the sound washed through her, making what she had to say to him all the more difficult. 'I don't do "entanglements" either. Far too messy and cumbersome. I'm interested in straightforward dating.'

'Elliot. This is no time for jokes.'

'I'm not making one, Sunainah.' He brushed the backs of his fingers down her cheek and smiled, finally giving in to the urge to touch her. How could he not? She was exquisite. 'I don't want to scare you, which is why I wanted to ascertain whether or not you felt the same powerful chemistry I do whenever we're alone like this.'

She slowly shook her head. 'It is…unexpected.'

'Wait.' Elliot looked at her in confusion. 'So you *do* feel it, too?'

'Yes, Elliot. I am aware of it existing between us but the point is that it cannot.'

'So all that ogling of my body earlier was for real?' he fished, and she found it difficult to hide a smile when he was like this. Teasing, gorgeous and incredibly sexy.

'Elliot, please, do not make this any more difficult than it already is.'

'What's so difficult? I want you. You want me.' He cupped her chin and raised it a little before brushing his thumb tantalisingly over her lower lip. Sunainah gasped at the contact, desperately wanting to touch his thumb with her tongue, to kiss his hand, to—

'Chemistry like this doesn't come along every day. You do realise that,' he felt compelled to point out as he continued to caress her mouth with his thumb, his

words slow and seductive. 'Spend time with me. Talk
to me. Let's get to know each other, Sunainah.'

Her knees were beginning to wobble even more than
before, and she tightened her grip on the door handle. When she didn't answer, he cupped her cheek and
looked down into her eyes, almost desperate to try and
figure out exactly what the road block was that was
stopping her from moving forward.

'Does it bother you that I have children? Is that why
you don't want to date me?'

'Why would it bother me?' She looked down at her
necklace then glanced at him. 'They are wonderful children and you are a wonderful father. It is beside the
point.'

'Which is?'

She sighed with exasperation. He really was not
going to let this subject go. 'Because you may find out
things about me that you do not like, and then I will
be upset and you will be upset and the children will be
upset, and it will make it uncomfortable at work, and
all of that can be avoided if we just remain colleagues
and neighbours.'

'What might I find out about you?'

Sunainah could not believe she had said as much as
she had, and as mortification started to flood through
her, her heart pierced with pain. Finding the strength
from somewhere, she opened the front door and rushed
outside, allowing the darkness of the night to envelop
her.

'Sunainah?' Elliot followed her.

'What are you doing? Go back inside to your children.'

'They're fine.' She was only a few steps in front of

him but thanks to his long legs he caught up to her in next to no time. He placed a hand on her shoulder, trying to stop her from walking away. 'Sunainah, wait.'

All she wanted to do was to get away, to reach the sanctuary of her home, where she could try and make some sort of sense of what was happening between them, but if she persisted in running, he might follow her all the way to her house. It was clear he was determined to get the answers he sought.

She stopped and turned to face him, pleased there was minimal light surrounding them now. It would make it easier to say what she had to say when she could not clearly see his handsome features. 'Elliot, I am not a good match for you.'

'I beg to differ. This attraction we feel…it's unique. We'd be fools to let this opportunity pass us by.'

'Then we will be fools.' There was firmness to her words.

'I'm sorry but I don't see that. It's just…' He broke off, deciding that he'd rather *show* her exactly how she made him feel, and without another word he closed the remaining distance between them, tenderly cupping one hand behind her neck, the other still holding her upper arm, although his grip was far from tight. He lowered his head and pressed his mouth to hers without further hesitation.

Sunainah gasped at the initial touch, stunned, shocked and surprised yet at the same time completely elated. Elliot was kissing her! *Her!*

His lips were not hard and firm, as she had expected, but rather soft and gently coaxing. She belatedly realised he was allowing her to control the kiss and for a split second she was not at all sure what to do. Then she realised that this might be her one and only chance to really experience what it might be like to be in Elliot's arms, to kiss him and to have him kiss her back. Had she not dreamed of a moment like this?

Slowly, she parted her lips, breathing in his intoxicating scent as she touched the tip of her tongue to his lower lip. A small delighted shudder rippled through him and she was flooded with a sense of feminine power. She had the ability to drive him to distraction and the knowledge magnified her desire for him.

With careful, deliberate movements, she slipped her hands around his waist, ever so pleased when he immediately reciprocated by wrapping his arms about her, holding her close, just as she had wanted. Safe, secure and yet incredibly sexy. Did the man have no clue how he made her feel?

Hearts pounding out a wild tattoo, she opened her mouth a little wider, wanting to tease him, wanting to show him just how intense the sensations between them were. There was no holding back, her hands rubbing in small circles at the base of his spine, her chest pressed against his firm torso and her mouth fulfilling every fantasy she'd had since they'd met.

She could feel his restraint about to snap at any moment and when she once more traced the outline of his mouth with her tongue, taking her time, memorising every contour, Elliot groaned with need.

'Sunainah.' Her name was a caress on his lips, and she adored the way he had said it. He truly did care about her, as was very evident from the way he was now kissing her back, enjoying getting to know her more intimately, just as she was doing with him.

It was a fantasy. She knew that just as she knew

fantasies never lasted, but as he plundered her mouth, still taking his time as though anxious to know every nuance of her mouth off by heart, Sunainah also knew she should put an end to this sooner rather than later.

'Elliot?' she tried, but he silenced her in the most perfect way possible, which only made rational thought that much more difficult. She did not want this to end but the truth of her situation was beginning to set off little warning bells all around her Elliot-filled senses.

She eased back, her breathing as harsh and erratic as his own.

'You taste like perfection,' he murmured.

'No. Please, do not say things like that.' Now that he was no longer kissing her, anguish, despair and shame flooded through her. What had she done? She broke free from his hold, hitched up the bag filled with paperwork and turned on her heel, heading towards her town house.

'Wait.' Elliot was hard on her heels, reaching for her hand and grasping her fingers. 'Wait. Sunainah. You can't just kiss me like that, turning my world upside down, and then walk away without a single word of explanation.'

'I can and I did. We are not suited.'

'I don't believe you and especially not after that intoxicating kiss we just shared.'

'It is not my problem what you do or do not believe.' She shifted away from his touch and continued walking towards her place, blinking rapidly when the front sensor light came on, bright and strong.

'Will you stop walking away from me?' He came after her. 'Honestly, you're the most exasperating and cryptic and frustrating woman I've ever met.' He shook his head and shoved both hands into the pockets of his khakis. 'If you want to deny how that kiss made you feel then go for it. Lie to yourself but don't think I'm going to do the same because I won't. That kiss was probably the most wonderful I've ever had in my life.'

'It was?' She stared at him for a moment before shaking her head, clearing the fog Elliot somehow always managed to stir within her.

'Yes. Please, Sunainah…just tell me why you're so certain we can't be together. Give me one good reason.'

Sunainah turned slowly to face him, ensuring she held his gaze while she said the words that would end their relationship before it had even begun.

'Just one,' he prompted, as she stood there, opening and closing her mouth like a goldfish.

Anguish ripped through her as she knew the only way to get through this was to just rip the sticking plaster off, to just blurt out what it was she knew she needed to say, even though she knew that once the words were said, they would wreck everything, they always did.

'We cannot do this, Elliot because…' She took in a deep breath, held it for a few seconds before letting it out. 'Because I am already married.'

CHAPTER SEVEN

ELLIOT WATCHED AS Sunainah entered her town house and closed the door without even turning to look back at him. He was stunned. Shocked. It took a full minute before he could even begin to process what she'd just said.

She was married?

How? Who?

'What?' Elliot wanted to bang on her door. He wanted to demand answers. She didn't wear a wedding ring. She didn't live with anyone. None of her friends had even alluded to a husband when they'd shared dinner or unpacked boxes or at any point since they'd met. How could Sunainah be married?

He took two steps towards her door then stopped. It was clear that her marriage was a touchy subject simply from the fact that it hadn't been raised until after he'd kissed her. What right did he have to ask her more questions?

He shook his head and exhaled with annoyance. Kissing Sunainah had been strange and marvellous and the most exhilarating thing he'd done in the past two years. At the back of his mind was a thread of guilt, guilt that he was cheating on Marie, that he *had* moved on with his life, but wasn't that what Marie had wanted?

Still, he'd never thought he would actually find another woman who made him feel so alive again. It was rare and he knew these sorts of feelings didn't come along every day. How could he be expected just to let all those emotions go, to let them vanish into thin air?

He'd taken a chance, he'd followed his gut instinct and he'd kissed Sunainah, and if the kiss had been any indication, it had been the right chance to take with the right woman.

His children adored her. Her patients adored her. Her staff respected her and her friends loved her. All in all, she was an amazing woman. She might be incredibly shy and introverted when it came to her private life but she was so strong and confident at the hospital. To say he was intrigued, that he was far more emotionally involved with Sunainah than he'd perhaps realised, was an understatement.

He'd leave it for now but he would also warn her that simply telling him she was married and then running away wasn't the end of the situation. If she *was* indeed married—and why would she lie about such a thing?— it was clear she wasn't *happily* married, or she wouldn't have kissed him the way she had.

No. This situation definitely required a bit more thought, a bit more care and a lot of finesse on his part not to spook or worry Sunainah. He wanted her to open up to him, to tell him the story of her past, to trust him. He wouldn't achieve that goal if he marched up to her door and demanded answers.

He would need to be patient, to let her know he was her friend first and foremost, and if she insisted on them maintaining a professional relationship then that's what he would do until she was comfortable.

Elliot eased back on his heels and crossed his arms over his chest as he continued to stare at her town house. Yes, he would show her he was a gentleman, that he would not rush her, but neither was he going to desert her, to ignore this frighteningly natural chemistry between them.

He blew a kiss to her darkened house then turned on his heel and slowly walked back towards his own home, deep in contemplation. He checked on both his children, pleased they were still sleeping soundly, unaware that their father's life had just taken a dramatic turn, but he knew in his heart it was a turn towards a positive future—a future he now wanted to share with Sunainah.

The next day, with his car now fixed, he was eager to get the children sorted out and dropped off at Grandma Liz's daycare centre so he'd have time before ward round to put the first step of his plan into action. By seven o'clock, fifteen minutes after he was supposed to have left his house, he was on his hands and knees, crawling under Daphne's bed looking for her favourite pair of sandals, which she was insisting on wearing. Stubborn and unwilling to compromise.

'You are such a girl, Daphne Marie,' he remarked once they'd eventually found the shoes at the bottom of the toy box. He picked her up and tickled her tummy with his nose, and Daphne squealed with delight. 'Some days, you really remind me of your mother. Determined but grateful.' He kissed her cheek before strapping her into her car seat.

At Grandma Liz's, he was delayed once more, trying not to let his impatience show when she asked him to check on two of the other children who were there. Elliot wanted to get to the hospital, he wanted to see Sunainah, he wanted to put his new plan into action, but he quickly reminded himself this was not a race he was running—it was a future direction that needed careful tweaking. He switched off his personal thoughts and pulled on his professional persona.

'They both felt quite hot to the touch,' Grandma Liz told him. 'Then again, they were both running around when they arrived, almost hyperactive, but in the last half an hour both of them seem to have had all their energy zapped out of them.'

'Are they from the same family?'

'No. Different families but they're friends and play together a lot.'

Elliot nodded dutifully, took the children into Liz's office and took their temperatures with the tympanic thermometer before looking at their throats and making them say, *'Ahh'*. He went through the normal checks and when he was finished, he frowned. 'They're definitely not one hundred per cent. Both have a slight fever and redness in the throat. Noses aren't runny. Eyes aren't glassy in appearance. Ears aren't red either.'

'Could it be a cold?' she asked.

Elliot continued to frown. 'Yes and no. I'd suggest calling their parents and having them sent home to rest. I know that's probably not what you wanted to hear but—'

'In places like this, germs spread easily.' Liz nodded. 'No. It's our policy to attempt to keep the spread of infection to a minimum. I'll do as you've prescribed and until their parents come to pick them up, I'll put them into a different room to separate them from the other children. Thank you, Elliot.'

'It's fine.'

'And yet you're still frowning,' Liz pointed out.

Elliot shook his head. 'It's just that Joshua wasn't well when we first moved here, which means his immune system is already susceptible to picking up whatever this might be.'

'Do you want to take him home today? I completely understand if that's the case.'

Elliot thought quickly. If he did take his children out of the daycare centre today, what was he supposed to do with them? He couldn't very well take them to the hospital with him and he had no other family he could drop them with. Neither could he take the day off work to stay with them.

'It should be fine. Just call me if Joshua—'

'I'll keep a close eye on him today.'

'Thank you. I'd appreciate that.' After kissing both of his children goodbye, and also putting his hand on Joshua's forehead just to check his son really was all right, Elliot left the daycare and finally headed towards the hospital, realising he'd already missed most of ward round.

As he walked past the A and E department, he heard someone call his name. It was Bergan. Trying not to roll his eyes, trying not to let his impatience show, trying to curb his need to see Sunainah's beautiful face once more, Elliot followed her.

'I'm glad I saw you walking in from the car park. Busy morning?'

'One of those that just doesn't want to let me get

to the ward,' he replied as they headed to treatment room one.

'I know those days. Anyway, here's the patient I'd like you to see,' she said, pulling back a curtain to reveal a small boy in the large bed, his mother standing by the boy's bedside, a worried expression on her face. Elliot did a quick visual examination of the boy, whose name was Pedro, as Bergan rattled off that the child had been complaining of headache, sore throat, earache and sore legs.

'Any vomiting?'

'No, but he feels hot,' Pedro's mother said. Even though the nurse had only recently taken the patient's temperature, Elliot took it again, noting it had risen in the last five minutes.

'Let me guess.' Sunainah's beautifully, modulated tones flooded the small treatment room as she glided in. 'High fever, sore ears, nose and throat and sore legs?'

Elliot tried not to stare, tried not to process the information that she was wearing another of her long professional skirts, which came to just below the knee. That her knit top was the most stunning shade of blue, that her hair, pulled back into its usual bun, looked incredibly sexy. Was it because he'd kissed her last night that she now looked completely different to him? He'd seen her dressed similarly before but now…

'Is that the case?' she asked, breaking into his wayward thoughts and thankfully returning his focus. What was it about this woman that enticed him so much? He was finding it difficult to remain professional.

'Yes.' Elliot looked back at Pedro, introducing him to Sunainah. 'It's the sore legs that concerns me most,' he said.

'Me as well,' she added, carefully feeling Pedro's legs for any sign of oedema. She glanced across at Elliot, watching as he reread the patient's notes, a small frown creasing his brow. 'Have you seen something like this before?'

Elliot shook his head. 'No, but it does remind me of something a colleague told me a few months ago.' He closed the case notes, trying to remember what he'd heard. 'What I'd suggest is admitting Pedro to the paediatric ward but in isolation.'

Pedro's eyes widened at this news but Elliot smiled reassuringly. 'It's all right, and it's just until we know exactly why you're in pain, we need to keep you separate from the other children. It's just a precaution.' He opened the notes again and took a pen from his top pocket.

'To begin with, I'd like scans of your legs, Pedro, to ensure there are no clots. We'll give you something to reduce the fever and you'll have a drip going into your arm to help keep your fluids up.'

Sunainah and Elliot spent a bit more time with Pedro and his mother, explaining what was going to happen, but after they left the treatment room Sunainah noticed Elliot was still frowning. Was this anything to do with her? About what she had said to him last night? About her marriage? Or was this solely about the patient?

She had not slept at all well and had woken with a headache. What must he think of her? She had not meant to kiss him last night, especially in such a wanton way. In fact, she had firmly decided to keep her emotional distance from him, to view him as a friend and colleague and nothing more, but the way his mouth had felt pressed against hers...the way she had felt his need for her and the way it had flattered her feminine senses were all things she should put right out of her mind—for ever.

She was not a free woman and although her marital situation was not of a typical nature, in the eyes of the law she was not permitted to kiss other men.

She had been dreading seeing Elliot this morning, knowing it was indeed inevitable, and when he had not turned up for ward round she had thought it something to do with her. As they walked back to the nurses' station so he could finish writing up his instructions for Pedro's treatment, she realised his mind was clearly on the problem of exactly what might be wrong with their patient.

'Sunainah.' Elliot stopped so suddenly in his tracks that she ploughed right into him. The immediate contact, the heat, the tingles, the sensory overload of accidentally touching him, one hand pressed flat against the firmness of his back as she quickly steadied herself, sent her senses into overload. She immediately looked up, directly into his wonderful blue eyes. His hand came around her waist, steadying her so they didn't topple over. He blinked once, glancing, oh, so briefly down at her mouth, the world around them completely slowing down.

'Er...sorry.' His lips barely moved as he spoke and within another second, after ensuring she wasn't going to fall, he dropped his hand back to his side, forcing himself to pull away. Slowly, slowly. First he had to earn Sunainah's trust, to let her see he was her friend. He walked to a chair and sat down, opening Pedro's notes.

Sunainah was surprised. Elliot was so calm and in control. Had he not felt that burning need that had roared to life between them the instant they had touched? Or was it simply the fact that now she had told him she was a married woman, that she was not free to indulge in a romantic relationship with him, he simply respected that fact and was behaving as a professional colleague should? If it was the latter, she should be pleased and yet… She closed her eyes, desperately trying to ignore the pang of pain that pierced her heart. Elliot had let her go. He didn't want her and she couldn't blame him.

He cleared his throat, bringing her attention back to the situation at hand. 'Sunainah, are there any other children in the ward with similar symptoms to Pedro's?'

Sunainah tried to clear her mind, tried not to focus on the warmth at her hip where she still felt the imprint of his hand. How could one simple, accidental touch wipe her mind completely blank? She stared at Elliot for one moment more, as though completely perplexed as to why she could not immediately recall the information he wanted.

'I know it's difficult to concentrate, Sunainah.' His words were soft, intimate, the way two doctors would often speak when not wanting their words to be overheard by others. There were nurses and radiographers and interns and clerical staff all around them and yet she felt certain no one else had heard his words to her. It was as though they really were in their own little world. 'I understand. I'm fighting, too, but we must… at least until we have time to sort out exactly what you said to me last night.'

'Oh!' So he was not going to let it go. He did want to know more but he was also correct that they needed to focus all their attention on Pedro and his symptoms, to ensure this wasn't the start of some new sort of epidemic.

'You rattled off Pedro's symptoms the instant you entered the treatment room. I take it there are others in the ward who are presenting with the same symptoms?'

'Yes. I did ask Nicole to move them all into the same ward room but I did not consider it might be some sort of epidemic…not until I saw that frown on your brow.'

Elliot nodded and quickly wrote up the treatment for Pedro. Then he asked one of the clerical officers if he could borrow her computer for a moment. He quickly searched for the name of the colleague who had told him about these odd symptoms.

'Ah…here it is. Daniel Tarvon.'

Sunainah looked at the image of Elliot's friend on the computer screen. 'Where does he work?'

'Mainly in Tarparnii.'

'That is one of the Pacific Islands, right? I have heard of it.'

'I worked with Daniel many years ago in Tarparnii.'

'Ah, yes. Pacific Medical Aid is the organisation that assists by sending medical teams over to help out.'

'Exactly. While I was there there was an outbreak of a disease called Yellom Cigru fever. The symptoms were similar…' Elliot continued click on different websites, looking through the lists of various medical research papers written by Daniel Tarvon and his wife, Melora.' He scrolled down through a list of symptoms, pointing them out. 'See?'

'But it says nothing about the sore legs. Why would everything be more ear, nose and throat related, symptoms of the common cold, but then adding sore and aching legs into the mix?'

'Exactly.' Elliot shook his head in frustration. 'I can't find what I'm looking for. I'll give Daniel a call and ask him my questions directly.'

'Is he still in Tarparnii?'

'I'm not sure. Possibly.' Elliot pulled out his cell phone, which was presently switched off as he was in A and E. 'Let's head up to the ward, examine the other patients more thoroughly, order more tests to figure out what we're really dealing with. The more information we can give Daniel, the better he'll be able to help us.'

'Good idea.' Sunainah nodded and as she walked alongside Elliot towards the paediatric ward he tried calling Daniel Tarvon but received only voice mail. He left a message. 'I'll call PMA as well. If Daniel's off in some remote jungle village, perhaps the only way to contact him will be via satellite phone.'

'Good idea. Thank you, Elliot.' As they turned the corner that led to the ward, she glanced up at him. 'I confess to being perplexed during ward round at the confusing symptoms being reported.'

'Sorry I missed it. Nothing seemed to go right this morning.'

Sunainah looked at him with concern as she opened the door to the ward. 'Daphne and Joshua? They are all right?'

'They're fine, but when I dropped them at daycare there were a few other children Liz wanted me to have a look at.'

'Did they show signs of these confusing symptoms?'

At Sunainah's words, Elliot stopped still in the middle of the ward. 'Actually, they did.'

Sunainah nodded. 'We should contact other hospitals and check. It might be nothing...'

'Or it might be something.'

'If these children at Grandma Liz's have these symptoms, what about Daphne and Joshua?' Sunainah was instantly worried about his gorgeous children. He could see it in her eyes and it warmed his heart to know she cared so much for them.

'Liz said she'd isolate the two children until their parents came to pick them up.'

'Do you want to go and get your children? Are you sure they will be OK? Joshua was sick only last week.'

'True. I would need to leave here and stay at home with the children.'

'Then that is what you do.'

'This whole single-parenting thing can sometimes be difficult to juggle.'

'Especially when children might be sick. I do understand but they are your first priority. I can always call in extra staff. Meanwhile, you can keep trying to track down your friend in Tarparnii and scour the internet for any information that might be helpful.'

He stepped closer to Sunainah, holding her gaze. 'I feel as though I'm leaving you in the lurch.'

'Everything will be fine.' Her words were soft, mainly due to his close proximity. Would she ever be able to stand near him without having her mind going blank and her body sparking to life with desire? 'Er...' She swallowed. 'We can talk on the phone and keep each other updated on progress.'

'OK.' He looked at her lips then back to her eyes, as though he wanted to seal the deal with a kiss, but knew it would definitely be the wrong thing to do. He eased back, putting distance between them. 'First, let's take a look at these other patients and order some tests. Then

I'll call Liz and tell her what might be happening.' He paused. 'I just don't want to panic her unnecessarily.'

'Grandma Liz is a wise woman. She does not have the "Grandma" in front of her name because it is an honorary title. She *is* a grandmother and she would prefer to err on the side of caution.'

'Good point.' Elliot nodded. 'Thank you, Sunainah. You always support me and I want you to know it's greatly appreciated.'

'That is my job, as colleague and neighbour.' *And as the woman who knows she is starting to fall in love with you*, she added silently as she offered him a small smile before turning and heading towards the ward room. Dealing with work would most definitely shift her thoughts back into alignment, and with Elliot at home with his children at least it provided her with some much-needed space.

Together they briefed Nicole on the latest events and assisted with setting up an isolation area in the ward. They ordered extra tests, the nurses took the extra blood samples and Sunainah and Elliot started explaining things to the worried parents.

'Right,' he said an hour later. 'I'll go collect my children. When I called Liz an hour ago, she said neither of them were showing symptoms.'

'That is good news, but it still is better to be safe than sorry.'

'Agreed. I'll let you know the instant I hear from Daniel. PMA has confirmed he headed off on a four-day drive to a distant village. They're going to track him down as soon as possible.'

'Good. I will let you know the test results the instant they come in. Now go. Look after your family.'

'I will. Thanks.' With a small smile in her direction and a brief lingering glance at her perfect mouth, as though he wanted nothing more than to press his lips to hers, Elliot turned on his heel and left the ward.

'Now, if a man looked at me the way he looks at you, I wouldn't be letting him walk out,' Nicole murmured from behind her. Sunainah spun round to stare at her friend, eyes wide with shock.

'What do you mean?'

'Oh, you know exactly what I mean. That man is very much into you, Sunainah. You should go for it. You deserve a good man like Elliot Jones.'

Sunainah opened her mouth to reply but closed it again, realising there was no point in having this discussion as it could never happen. She and Elliot were destined to be colleagues and neighbours, nothing more, so it would serve her better if she simply ignored the way his brief glance had left her body trembling with repressed delight.

'I will be in my office, juggling the staffing rosters. Two nurses need to pick up their children from childcare. The hospital daycare centre is on high alert for symptoms and other hospitals are also starting to report incidences of these confusing symptoms.'

'Only reports of children?' Nicole's tone was tinged with serious concern.

'At this stage.' Sunainah sighed, wanting Elliot to get hold of his friend Daniel Tarvon immediately. If his friend could shed any light on the symptoms, it would be a blessing, especially before things became any worse.

Four more cases were admitted to the paediatric ward before the end of the day and Sunainah had never spoken more to Elliot, the two of them keeping in close contact via phone and email. She had sent him the test results, all reporting no signs of blood clots but definite spikes in white-cell production. The sick children were on intravenous drips and analgesics to reduce their fevers.

'Are you heading home to rest?' Elliot asked later that night. 'You'll probably sleep better in your own bed.'

'I was thinking of it.'

'Will's going to be at the hospital. He's a good doctor. He'll call if there are any changes. Rest and refresh your mind. Come home, Sunainah.'

'Come home?' she queried as she eased back in her office chair and closed her eyes. Did he want her to sleep at his place? To be there when he received the call from his friend?

'To the cul-de-sac, I meant.' But even as he spoke he could not remove the intimacy from his tone as the image of Sunainah walking into his home, being enveloped in his arms, the two of them sleeping in the same bed… Elliot stopped his thoughts. She was married. She had told him she was married and while he wanted nothing more than to quiz her on this topic, now was not the time.

'Oh.' She sighed. 'Yes. I think you are right. I am tired.'

'It's been a long day and tomorrow may be longer. Rest.'

'Yes.' Sunainah opened her eyes and rose from her chair. 'I shall lock my office, say goodnight to the staff and head home.'

'Call me when you arrive, just so I know you're home

safe. I'm in a worrying kind of mood,' he added, as though to justify his comment.

'All right.'

'I'll speak to you later, then.' With that he rang off.

Sunainah looked at her phone for a moment before smiling and slowly shaking her head. It was nice to have someone worrying about her again. It was one thing she had missed once her father's dementia had become worse. Her father had always tried to do his best to protect her, to care for her and to worry about her.

As she finished at the hospital, telling the staff to call if there was any change, no matter how small or insignificant, she headed home. When she drove past Elliot's town house, she noticed one of the downstairs lights was on. Elliot was obviously in his office, hopefully talking to Daniel Tarvon and getting some answers. They had both scoured the internet as best they could, reread articles from medical journals, discussed and consulted with other personnel from different specialities, hoping someone, somewhere had some sort of clue about what they were dealing with.

For now, though, most of the children who had reported with these strange symptoms were stabilising, but no one knew for how long. It was the unknown that concerned her most. What if these symptoms were only the beginning and things were about to get worse? What then?

Sunainah garaged her car and headed inside, opening her fridge to look for something she could eat. She had her phone in her hand and was just about to call Elliot to report that she was home safely when it rang. Elliot's name coming up on the screen.

'Did you see my car headlights go past your ho—?'

'Sunainah? Quick. Come quick. It's Joshua. He has a fever. He has the symptoms. Sunainah?' There was panic in his voice, panic she had most certainly never heard before. 'Sunainah?' His voice broke. 'I don't know what to do. It's my son. *My* son!'

CHAPTER EIGHT

SUNAINAH FOUND THE front door open as she entered his town house.

'Elliot!' she called, racing through to Joshua's downstairs bedroom, unable to believe her own level of anxiety. Was Joshua as bad as Elliot thought? What if they could not figure out the correct treatment in time? Her heart pounded with fear as her mind raced through several different scenarios.

When she entered Joshua's bedroom she breathed a sigh of relief when she saw Elliot sitting in the rocking chair, holding a Joshua in his arms, a cold face washer to the little boy's forehead. 'How high is his temperature?'

'Thirty-eight point seven. I've given him paracetamol but…but…' Elliot looked up at her, anguish in his eyes. 'I don't know what to do, Sunainah.' He pressed a kiss to the little boy's head. 'He's my boy. *My boy.*'

'I know, and I am here to help you.' She placed a hand on his shoulder and looked into his eyes. It did not matter what might or might not happen in the future between the two of them—right now they were a team. 'We will get through this together. That is what friends do.'

He looked up at her and nodded, his eyes sombre and filled with concern for his son. 'After Marie's death he was so sick but he fought back and won.'

'He is a fighter.' She nodded as she put down the emergency medical kit she had brought with her and reached for her stethoscope. 'Let me have a look at him. Put him in his cot and go and refresh the face washer. Get it nice and cool.'

'Yes. Yes.' Elliot was pleased to be given orders and did as he was told while Sunainah quickly examined Joshua. He definitely had the same signs and symptoms as the other children in the paediatric ward but at this stage, he was not too bad.

'Thank goodness your father knew what signs to look out for,' she told the little boy calmly as she stroked his cheek. 'It will be all right, Joshua. Daddy and I will look after you.'

'Nen-nah,' he whimpered, and Sunainah's heart turned over with love for the little boy.

'Nen-nah's here, sweet one.' She sighed as she rubbed her fingers gently on his legs. 'Are your legs sore?'

He grizzled a bit and nodded but he did not flinch from her gentle touch. That was a good sign. Joshua looked at her with his big blue eyes, so much like his father's. 'We will get you sorted out.' She bent and pressed a kiss to his hot forehead, unable to believe just how precious he was to her. Elliot returned, cool face washer in hand, and immediately pressed it to Joshua's skin.

'His symptoms are still mild, which means you caught it nice and early.' She smiled reassuringly at him. 'Good job, Daddy.' Sunainah spoke quietly as they stood by Joshua's cot, watching the little boy as he dozed. 'We should check to see if Mackenzie and John can look after Daphne.'

'He needs to go to hospital?'

'It will be best if he is there. We can start him on a drip to replace fluids.'

'Yes. Dehydration is the one thing we don't want. Yes, you're right.' Elliot breathed out and before Sunainah knew what was happening he had enveloped her in his arms. 'Thank you, Sunainah. I feel as though my brain is beginning to return.'

His words were spoken next to her ear, his voice deep, the vibrations tingling through her body, which was half pressed against his. She knew the embrace was more from relief than of a sensual nature but she could not help the way her body responded to his every time he was so close to her.

She forced herself to speak, to say something normal because it would help her to stop wanting to snuggle closer to him. 'Mackenzie also worries whenever Ruthie is sick. Thankfully, her husband usually keeps cool and calm.'

'So now I have you to settle my mind and bring me back to a more respectable level of parental freak-out.' He chuckled softly and she was pleased he had relaxed enough to laugh. That was a good thing as it would release some of his stress and tension. Her own stress and tension, however, was still mounting as he continued to hold her, both of them standing there watching Joshua's steady breathing as though they were a proper couple, raising two children together.

Sunainah knew she needed to move, to put some distance between them, and soon because if he turned and looked down into her upturned face she knew she

would kiss him without hesitation. She was almost positive she was falling in love with him and that was fine
so long as she did not lead him on. She would have to
figure out a way to cope with loving him yet working
alongside him day after day as nothing more than a colleague and friend. Standing in his arms like this might
give him false hope, and she simply was not that mean.

She eased back from his embrace and Elliot immediately dropped his arms, quickly shoving his hands
into the pockets of his jeans. He looked contrite and a
little bit hurt and she was not sure why.

'Well, at least I'm not the only parent who freaks
out when their kid is sick,' he remarked as he took a
step away from her, turning his full attention back to
his son. 'Would you mind calling Mackenzie? I'll pack
a bag for Joshie. We can take him in my car. No need
for an ambulance.'

'Of course.'

Elliot continued to look at his son, trying not to think
how wonderful it had been to hold Sunainah close. The
woman fitted perfectly into his arms and it was clear she
honestly cared for his children, but the fact remained
that Sunainah wasn't free for him to hug whenever he
wanted to.

He kept his gaze trained on Joshua as he heard Sunainah leave the room, talking softly on her cell phone to
Mackenzie. Her tones, the lilt of her words, her accent
usually had such a soothing effect on him yet tonight
all it was doing was reminding him that she couldn't
be a part of his life.

He'd been ready to take a step forward, to really
move away from his past life with Marie. 'Until death
us do part' were the words he'd vowed, and when death

had parted them he'd felt as though his life had been plunged into turmoil. Yet by some miracle, he'd met another woman, one who was driving him to distraction with longing, wanting and needing.

There was so much he didn't know about Sunainah, so much he wanted to know, and the unanswered questions were driving him crazy. He needed to be patient, to wait until Joshua's health was improving and then he would sit down with Sunainah and figure everything out. He had to chance it, had to believe that all of these 'coincidences' that had happened around them actually meant something more.

'It's all right, little man. We'll figure everything out in time,' he told his son. 'Daddy's here.' And that would have to be enough for now, even though it was all too easy to cast Sunainah in the role of surrogate mother.

'Mackenzie is coming over immediately,' she told him from the doorway. Now that Joshua was stabilising and the immediate alarm had disappeared, Elliot appeared more calm. It was a good sign. 'She will take Daphne to her place, if that is all right with you.'

'It's fine. Thank you.'

'Would you like me to wake Daphne?'

'Yes. I'll stay with Joshie.'

'As you wish.'

He heard her head upstairs and closed his eyes for a moment. 'I shouldn't have been so direct with her,' he told Joshua as he once again checked his son's temperature. 'No change! What on earth is this thing?'

Joshua started to cry again and put both hands on his legs. Elliot's heart turned over with empathetic pain. 'What is it? What's causing this?' He was annoyed that he didn't know. 'Think. *Think*.' He picked his son up, holding the boy close, hoping the feel of his father's big, strong arms would somehow help to ease the pain. His emotions were all over the place tonight and when he turned and saw Sunainah standing in the door, a sleepy Daphne in her arms, he shrugged his shoulders. 'I feel so helpless.'

'We will sort it out. I promise you.'

'Hello? Elliot? Sunainah?' Mackenzie's voice came from the doorway and Sunainah offered Elliot a comforting smile before she went to greet her friend. Within ten minutes Daphne was settled at Mackenzie's, and Sunainah was driving Elliot's car to the hospital. Elliot sat in the back seat next to Joshua's car seat, monitoring his son's condition.

'You're doing great,' he encouraged Sunainah as she drove his large family car towards the hospital. 'I'm sorry you didn't get a chance to rest.'

'I am fine,' she told him. 'I have coped with less sleep before now.'

'Haven't we all.' His words were wry and when she looked at him in the rear-vision mirror, she saw the corners of his mouth turned up, just slightly. They were only a few minutes from the hospital when Elliot's cell phone rang. The noise startled poor Joshua, who whimpered and tried to move, but his body was listless. Sunainah kept looking at him in the rear-vision mirror, her heart pouring out to him.

'It's all right, buddy,' Elliot soothed, his eyes lighting with relief as he noted the caller was Daniel Tarvon.

'Tarvon. Thank goodness,' he said, switching the call to loudspeaker so Sunainah could hear what was being said. 'We have children here with a variety of symptoms and I wanted to pick your brains.'

'Pick away,' Daniel offered, and listened intently to what Elliot was saying. 'Ah. Yes, yes. We've had outbreaks here. First seen just a few months ago by one of our German PMA doctors. He's called it Hergeldorct Tela fever and it's a new strain of Yellom Cigru found predominantly in pre-pubescent children.

'It can be identified by the horrendous pain in the legs. Other than that, it presents with either cold or flu symptoms, sometimes with high fever and vomiting, but for some reason, which our German colleague is still doing tests on, it affects the legs, and that's why there isn't much literature available at the moment. Tests are still inconclusive.'

'Treatment?' Sunainah asked as she turned into the hospital's emergency bay.

'Initial injection of non-steroidal anti-inflammatory drugs into both quadriceps for the leg pain, then elevate legs above the heart. As it's not bacterial, antibiotics won't work but a course of regular paracetamol will reduce fever and the usual intravenous drip will replenish fluids.'

Elliot ran his hand over Joshua's forehead before kissing it. 'You're going to get better, buddy. Daddy's going to make you better.'

'Your son has the fever?' Tarvon asked.

'Yes. We're just pulling up at the hospital.'

'Go. Treat them,' Tarvon said. 'I'll stay by the satellite phone if you need any further information.'

'Thanks, mate.' Elliot rang off as Sunainah pulled up near one of the ambulance bays. An orderly came out to see what was happening and she quickly tossed him Elliot's car keys.

'Sunainah?' The orderly seemed surprised, even

more so when Elliot climbed from the back of the car
with a sick boy in his arms.

'Would you please park Elliot's car, Douglas?'
Sunainah asked as she followed Elliot into A and E.

'I'm taking him directly to the ward. I can't admit
him as I'm his father but—'

'I will admit him,' she replied, placing a hand on his
elbow, wanting to reassuring him in his time of need.
'Let us go there directly and—'

'Sunainah?'

Sunainah turned when she heard someone call her
name. Her friend Bergan came rushing towards her.

'I was just about to have you paged. I've had two
more children brought in.' Bergan beckoned for her to
follow. Sunainah looked from her friend back to Elliot.

'Go. I'll get things started.'

'Yes. We must get these treatments started.' But as
they walked away in opposite directions, Sunainah's
heart yearned to be with Elliot, to ensure Joshua was
indeed all right. She loved that little boy as though he
were her own.

And his father? She closed her eyes for a moment, re-
calling the way she had felt in his arms, with his mouth
pressed to hers. So perfect. So right. A few weeks ago
she had not even known Elliot and Joshua and Daphne
existed but now she could not bear to be parted from
that little family. Was this normal?

She shook her head, knowing she had to find a way
to put her personal thoughts on hold so she could focus
on her job. So many of her patients needed her right
now and she owed it to all of them, not just Joshua, to
do her best to treat them. She followed Bergan, pleased

she now had a treatment plan to follow, hoping Tarvon's information was correct.

As she administered the medication and stood watch over the two patients in A and E, waiting for them to show signs of stabilising, of the pain in their legs to decrease, of the fever to start dropping, she managed to call the paediatric ward so she could at least get an update on Joshua.

'Temperature has dropped half a point and he's not whimpering in pain any more.' Elliot's smooth voice came down the line, washing over Sunainah and renewing her strength.

She sighed with relief. 'That is excellent news. My two patients here are showing similar signs. I am about to arrange their transfer to the ward.'

'Good. Good.'

Sunainah closed her eyes, allowing his warm, rich tones to wash over her. It was a selfish thing to do but she needed it. 'You sound more at ease.' Talking to Elliot, being near him, working alongside him had the ability to strengthen her. Yes, she was indeed most selfish because she wanted these sensations to continue for ever.

'I am. Joshie is picking up. Mackenzie sent me a text to say Daphne is sleeping soundly in the spare bed in Ruthie's room so at least I know she's all right too.'

'I am happy to hear it.'

'Plus, there's you.'

'Me?'

'I can cope better with things like sick children when you're near me.'

'Oh?' At his words, her heart rate, which felt as though it had only just settled into a more normal rhythm, began to beat double time against her chest. She was glad she was sitting down and that there were not too many of the nursing staff around her at the moment, providing her with a bit of privacy.

'Sunainah, I want you to know that I've heard what you've said, that you're…married, but I also know there's a lot more to this story than you're telling me. But I want you to know that I'm not easily scared. With what I've been through these past few years, watching Marie die, having her family blame me for her death, entrusting them with Daphne, only to be hauled into court to be told I wasn't a good father, I've realised I'm a lot stronger than I thought.' His voice had dropped to a more intimate level and her heart pierced with pain at his words.

'Just when I thought things couldn't get any worse, they did, but that's all in the past. It's been dealt with and I know Marie would have been terribly hurt had she seen the behaviour of her parents and sisters, with the way they were desperate to have Daphne live with them because it was the only way they knew how to hold on to a part of their daughter. I can understand the psychology behind their actions but on an emotional level it was imperative for me to leave town, to uproot my children, to leave my friends and colleagues and start again.

'And then I met you.' He paused. 'I've felt love before, Sunainah. My marriage, although short, was a happy one, and while I will always love Marie, I also know she didn't want me to be alone. Not only that, she told me to find someone special to help me raise the children.'

'Elliot—'

'Just a moment. Hear me out. I want you to know that whatever this is…this thing between us, Sunainah, I'm very interested. My children think the world of you, especially Joshua. He does not like strangers, doesn't like people he doesn't know holding him and yet the very first time we met he went to sleep in your arms.'

'He was not well,' she felt compelled to point out.

'Even so, it was very out of character for my little man, but now I see that he was right all along. His actions showed me you were indeed someone to be trusted, someone who was very caring and giving and loving. That's rare and special.' He exhaled slowly and she could imagine him up in the quiet ward, leaning back in one of the chairs at the nurses' station, his eyes closed as he spoke quietly to her on the phone.

'I felt horrible leaving Daphne tonight, palming her off on Mackenzie and John, and even though I know she's fine and she's happy, I still feel guilty, Sunainah. I could have brought her with us to the hospital but then I wouldn't have been able to give one hundred per cent of my attention to Joshua, who needed me. I know I'm fortunate to have such wonderful neighbours and, believe me, I appreciate that more than I can say, but I still feel guilty. I left her behind before and I want to make sure I never do it again.'

Sunainah's heart felt his pain, his anguish, and she recalled similar words from her father, words it had taken him well over two decades to confess to her.

'You've been too sheltered,' her father had once said when she had spent yet another night playing card games with him and finishing off a jigsaw puzzle. 'You should be going out. Having fun. Meeting people your own age. Meeting men. Getting married. Having a family of your own.'

'I am fine, Father.'

Her father had shaken his head, his tone filling with repressed emotion. 'I should have taken better care of you, Sunainah.'

'You did. You took excellent care of both my mother and myself.' Sunainah had placed her hand on her father's shoulder. 'We were happy.'

She had not wanted to point out that she could not get married as she was already legally married, because it was a subject on which her father had confessed to feeling his greatest failure. Not only the failure, as he had seen it, of protecting his daughter from the cultural tradition of arranged marriages but also of getting the marriage annulled.

For so long neither of them had spoken of it, and as her father's dementia had increased, he had become muddled as to whether he had finally achieved his goal of 'rescuing' his daughter's honour. She had always thought he had 'taken care of' things, as he had promised her, and it had only been when she and Raj had filed the paperwork for a marriage licence that she had discovered she was still married. That had been five years ago and she remained wed to a man in India she barely knew.

Sunainah hated to think about that time in her life, of her forced marriage to Amir. It was filled with too much pain and confusion as well as the terror of being a fourteen-year-old girl married off to thirty-five-year-old man. It had not been her father's fault and she had never blamed him. When he had discovered what Sunainah's grandfather had done he had most certainly come to her rescue, whisking her back to his home country of England. She had never returned to India and she did not want to.

Yes, she wanted Elliot to protect Daphne and to continue to protect his daughter for the rest of the little girl's life, but in the light of tonight's events it had been the logical course of action to ensure Daphne was not only safe with Mackenzie and John but also happy. Knowing Daphne and the way she not only loved her brother but with her need to always help, the little girl might have been distraught to know Joshua was sick.

'You did the right thing, leaving her with Mackenzie,' Sunainah offered after a long moment of silence. 'And I want you to know you are a good father, Elliot.'

'Even though I'm constantly second-guessing myself? Even though I fell to pieces when Joshua's temperature spiked?'

'Yes. It is because you are second-guessing yourself that you are a good father. All parents worry about their children and they all show it in different ways. Remember Mr Preedy? How he blustered and bullied because he thought little Rory was not getting any better?'

'I hope I'm not that bad.'

Sunainah chuckled and opened her eyes, feeling the intense emotions Elliot had evoked within her beginning to subside to a more normal level. 'You are not, thank goodness.'

'You, lady, are good for my ego.'

She laughed again and sat up straighter in the chair. 'I had better go and check on my patients and then I will come up to the ward. I have already jotted down some notes for a protocol document to be sent to the other hospitals about the treatment Tarvon has suggested. From what I can see, it definitely appears to be working.'

'Agreed. The sooner treatment can begin the better, and that can only happen if all staff know what signs and symptoms to be looking for. OK. I'll go check on Joshua and the other patients and I'll see you when you come up.' He paused, then, before he rang off, he said, 'Thanks for listening to me, Sunainah.'

'It is my pleasure,' she told him, not at all surprised when a warm blush of happiness seemed to envelop her. A few sweet, appreciative words from Elliot and she was once more reduced to mush. He rang off and Sunainah slowly put the receiver down as Bergan walked into the A and E nurses' station.

'Everything all right?' Bergan asked.

'Yes. Yes, Elliot's son is doing much better.'

'I meant is everything all right with *you*?' Bergan clarified.

Sunainah looked into the eyes of her friend, a woman who had been through a lot of heartbreak and hardship herself, and knew she could not fob Bergan off with placating words. 'I am confused and concerned and...'

'Falling for Elliot?'

Sunainah gasped in shock. 'You can tell?'

Bergan smiled and gave her friend a quick hug. 'We're all here for you, Sunainah. Mackenzie, Reggie and I. Whatever you need. Navigating the rocky path of love can be pretty tricky but...' Bergan sighed in a romantic way, her gaze straying to just past Sunainah where Richard was standing. 'It's worth it. Well worth it.'

Richard walked over and slipped his arm around Bergan's waist, pressing a quick kiss to her lips. 'There's my wife.' He looked at Sunainah and winked. 'Nothing like working side by side with the woman you love.' He returned his attention to Bergan. 'Ready? The drop-in youth centre is awaiting our presence.'

'Almost,' Bergan said, and looked at Sunainah. 'You're fine getting the treatment plan for Hergeldorct Tela fever out to other hospitals?'

'Yes. Elliot and I will take care of it and ensure it is posted up on the relevant online bulletin boards. You two go. I must get to the ward.' Sunainah smiled at her friends and headed off to the ward, still unused to seeing Bergan looking so happy.

Was she right? Were these confusing emotions she felt for Elliot really worth fighting for? What if it led her down the path of pain? She had been there before with Rajesh. He had said he would look after her, he had promised they would have a long and happy life together, and then he had broken her heart when he had discovered her past.

Would Elliot be able to cope with what had happened to her? With the details of her marriage and the fact that she was emotionally powerless to deal with it?

The instant she entered the paediatric ward Elliot greeted her with a large, beaming smile and for just a moment all her doubts fled. When she looked into his eyes, when she was standing near him and having him smile at her in such an all-encompassing way, she truly believed she could handle anything. He took her hand in his and pulled her towards the far end of the ward where Nicole had set up an isolation area.

'Come and see him, Sunainah. He's doing so much better. Come and see.' Elliot was so happy. 'After I got

off the phone to you I checked on him and the other patients and it was just…spectacular.'

He tugged her along with him impatiently, and she
couldn't help but smile at the change in his mood. Here
was not only a doctor who was pleased the treatment
had worked but a father who was elated his son's condition was improving in leaps and bounds.

They entered the isolation area where several of the
young children who had been afflicted with the odd
symptoms of Hergeldorct Tela fever were starting to
improve.

'The treatment is most definitely working.' She nodded as she waved to some of her patients who were now
able to sit up in their beds before heading over to where
Joshua was lying in his cot. Her smile increased as she
looked down at him, and when he held his arms up to
her, indicating he wanted her to pick him up, she could
not help the tears that came to her eyes.

'I told you he was feeling better.' Elliot, filled with
fatherly pride, stood next to her as she carefully picked
Joshua up from his cot, mindful of the IV drip in the
little boy's arm. The instant Joshua was close, she closed
her eyes and buried her face in his cute little neck,
breathing in the life that was surrounding him.

'Oh, Joshua. We were so worried,' she whispered,
knowing the little boy would not completely understand her words. 'You are so precious, little one.' She
dropped a kiss on his head then opened her eyes, surprised to find Elliot watching her with great interest.
He nodded, as though satisfied with her response, his
deep blue eyes filled with delight.

Sunainah found herself unable to move, looking at
him looking at her. She was holding his son as though

she were the boy's mother, and that did not seem to bother Elliot one little bit. Indeed, all he did was step closer and put his arm around her shoulders, drawing her closer as Joshua snuggled further into her arms.

'Thank you, Sunainah.' His words were barely above a whisper, and as she continued to look up into his face, her heart hammering wildly against her ribs, she had the fleeting thought that Elliot might actually kiss her, right here, in the ward, in front of everyone.

She blinked once then swallowed, her lips parting slightly as she suddenly realised she wouldn't care if he did. In fact, to feel his mouth pressed to hers once more would be absolutely perfect because her heart was presently hammering out his name.

Joshua shifted, trying to get more comfortable in her arms, and it was his small movements that brought Sunainah out of the wonderful dream. She edged away from Elliot, murmuring softly that she had best put Joshua back in his cot so he could continue to rest.

When she was near Elliot she felt confused. When she was apart from him she felt confused. Would there ever be a day when the confusion would lift and she would receive some level of understanding as to exactly what was happening to her?

They spent a few more minutes with Joshua then Sunainah checked on the other patients, pleased the treatment was most definitely working. Every time she moved she was highly conscious of Elliot's presence, wondering whether he had felt that same undercurrent of desire that had pulsed through her.

'I had better go and write up the treatment proto-col for the other hospitals to follow,' she remarked as she left the isolation area, unable to meet Elliot's gaze.

What had he seen as they'd stood there, staring at each other, his son in her arms? Had he seen just how much his son meant to her? That she cared for him more than she did for her other patients? Did he see that she was happy because *his* son was getting better? Heaven forbid he realise that his nearness, his close-ness, the touch of his arm about her shoulders, binding them together into one unit, was a dream she wished would come true.

She almost raced to her office, needing some space, some privacy, some hope of finding peace with the mul-titude of confusing emotions pulsing through her.

It's worth it. Well worth it. Bergan's words repeated in Sunainah's mind as she sat behind her desk and switched on her computer. Was it? What would hap-pen when Elliot found out the truth about her marriage? Would he understand? Would he think it ridiculous or old-fashioned? Would he blame her for her cowardice in refusing to deal with the entire situation?

She forced her wayward thoughts back into line and began typing up the necessary information for the treat-ment of Hergeldorct Tela fever and emailed it to the nec-essary online medical bulletin boards, as well as to the other hospitals who had reported cases of the condition. She also noticed that Pacific Medical Aid, the company with which Daniel Tarvon and his German colleague worked, had also put information up on their website.

She scanned it quickly but now her thoughts kept returning to the way Elliot had looked at her. The way he had held her close.

She closed her eyes, unable to believe the security she had felt in Elliot's arms. What had she been think-ing? Elliot had come here to start a new life, to give his children a fresh start, and she was sure that would not include becoming embroiled in her own problems. He did not need that stress in his life. This was her burden to carry. She had been doing it for so long now it was second nature to her, but to try and explain it to—

She jumped as the door to her office opened. Elliot came in, closing the door quietly behind him. Sunainah stood, a question on her lips, but she had no chance to ask it as Elliot covered the remaining distance between them, scooped her into his arms and pressed his mouth to hers.

CHAPTER NINE

NOTHING ELSE MATTERED except the feeling of being in Elliot's arms, of the enticing way his mouth was creating havoc with her senses. It felt so right, so perfect to be with him like that, and the thought that it would all end when he finally learned the truth about her filled her with despair.

She clung to him, matching his need with perfect synchronicity. How was it possible to feel such powerful emotions and know them to be wrong? As the combined heat between them began to rise, Elliot shifted slightly, bringing his hands up to the nape of her neck, where he started pulling the pins from her hair, throwing them heedlessly on the floor until her hair had been pulled from the band and was floating freely around her shoulders.

He plunged his fingers into the long, silky locks, moaning with delight at the sensations she was evoking in him. Now that his son was improving and out of danger, all he had been able to think about was how perfect Sunainah had looked holding his son. It had already become abundantly clear to him that Joshua and Daphne thought the world of her but seeing her cradling his sick son, smiling at him with a mother's love, had stirred something deep and primal within Elliot.

He knew she'd told him she was married but that hadn't stopped him from following through on his need to haul her close and kiss her. He didn't care what the truth of the situation was; the realisation that she belonged with him was something he was willing to fight for. Whoever her husband was, wherever he was, Elliot would do whatever he could to ensure Sunainah was freed from the relationship she clearly wasn't attached to, so the two of them could be together.

The fact that she had instantly kissed him back the moment his mouth had touched hers gave him confidence that she was as smitten with him as he was with her. She was intoxicating him to the point where logical and rational thought were irrelevant.

What mattered was the taste of her lips, the sweet scent of her skin, the silkiness of her hair, the gorgeous curves of her body. The woman fitted perfectly in his arms and as he continued to run his fingers through her hair Elliot knew he should make some sort of attempt to slow things down, to ensure he didn't scare her. She deserved to be cherished.

He'd already guessed Sunainah wasn't very experienced when it came to men, that she was shy and reserved, but with the way her mouth was matching the urgency of his, the same burning desire coursing through her, perhaps he had been mistaken. How could she be married and still give the sense that she was an innocent?

Her hands had automatically gone around his waist, her fingers rubbing tantalising circles on his back. It was a small action but one that was driving him even more insane with longing and need. How could it be possible that this woman who fitted so perfectly into his arms, who kissed him back with what felt like all the passion in her soul, who could pierce his soul with one simple look, could be married to someone else?

'Sunainah.' Elliot's mouth broke away from hers as suddenly as he had captured it. His breathing was harsh and uneven, which made her feel a little better as she gasped for air. How was it possible she had failed to show restraint a second time? What must he think of her? Did it lower his opinion of her, that she would kiss him back in such a wanton way when she had already confessed to not being free to do such a thing?

'Sunainah.' He breathed her name again as he put his hands on her shoulders, making sure there was at least an arm's distance between them. He stared at her, looking at her for the first time with her long, black hair floating gloriously around her shoulders and down her back. He gasped and slowly shook his head from side to side.

'Do you have any idea just how stunning you are? How you can tie me in knots with just one look?' His words were deep yet soft and a fresh wave of desperate need and longing flooded through her. 'You are so incredibly beautiful and elegant and kiss like a dream, but you *have* to explain to me how you came to be married? I just don't understand.'

She continued to stare into his eyes, waiting for her breathing to slowly return to normal, but it was doing no such thing. 'You think I am beautiful?'

He laughed with disbelief. 'How can you not know how gorgeous you are?'

'Because no one has ever really told me.'

'Not even this husband of yours?'

She shook her head, closing her eyes at the mention of the man who had effectively wrecked her life. She knew she owed Elliot an explanation, especially after the heart-thumping kiss they had just shared.

'No. He—' She broke off and turned away from him before opening her eyes. She walked over to the window and stared out unseeingly into the darkness of the night.

He crossed to her side and placed his hands on her shoulders, gently turning her to face him. 'I know this is probably very difficult for you but I need to know.'

'Of…of course.' She looked directly at his mouth as she spoke, unable to stop the way her mind did not want to focus on anything other than having him repeat that glorious kiss over and over again. She licked her lips and he groaned, and her gaze immediately flicked up to meet his.

'Don't look at me like that.'

'I cannot help it,' she confessed, tipping her head forward, momentarily pleased he had released her hair from its bonds as it now provided the perfect shield for her. It seemed pointless to deny just how wonderful he made her feel, how incredible it had been to be held so closely to him, to feel cherished and wanted and…loved?

No. It could not be possible that Elliot loved her. She was not the sort of woman men fell in love with. They appreciated her, perhaps they even admired her from time to time, but men did not fall in love with a forty-year-old workaholic who had spent most of her adult life working hard to complete her studies while caring for her sick parents.

Elliot groaned again and dropped his hands from her

shoulders, shoving an unsteady hand through his hair. 'I'm at the stage where I'm not sleeping properly because all I can think about is you.' He shook his head.

'I am sorry, Elliot.'

'Don't be sorry, Sunainah.' He looked at her, his gaze tender. 'Don't ever be sorry for the way you make me feel because I haven't felt this way in a very long time.' He was by her side in an instant, brushing his knuckles gently down her cheek. 'I came here for a fresh start, not only for the children but for myself. I thought perhaps one day I might meet someone new.' A slow smile spread across his lips. 'I never thought it would be so soon.'

'Elliot.' She closed her eyes, as though even just saying his name was causing her deep consternation and pain. 'Please do not say things like that.' She shook her head. 'I do not deserve someone like you.'

'How can you say that?' Elliot cupped her face, and she reluctantly opened her eyes and stared into his. 'Sunainah? Please tell me. Tell me about your marriage.'

She held his gaze, knowing there was no way for her to move forward with her life without confessing to Elliot the particulars of her past. She knew once Elliot realised her predicament, he would leave her alone. He would find another woman who would no doubt help to fill the void in his life, to be there for him on a day-to-day basis, to help him raise his wonderful children. The thought caused pain to rip through her, to dig its claws deep into her heart and begin the process of dismantling her hope.

He bent his head and brushed a soft and tantalising kiss across her lips. 'For courage,' he murmured, that gorgeous, small smile touching his mouth in the way she would often dream about.

'I do not know…how to tell you.' Either way she was going to lose him. She closed her eyes for a moment, needing to gather her thoughts, and she could not do that when he was looking at her with such intense encouragement.

Elliot dropped his hands from her face but where she thought he might walk away, putting more distance between them, she discovered she was wrong as he linked his hands with hers, giving her fingers a little squeeze of encouragement. 'Would it help if I asked you questions?'

She opened her eyes but this time could not look at him, hanging her head a little as the pain of the situation she tried so hard to forget, to push aside, began to impact on her mind. 'Perhaps.'

'OK.' He reached out a hand and tenderly pushed her hair behind her ear so he could see her face more clearly. 'Where is your husband?'

'I do not know.' As she spoke the words, shame began to wash over her.

'Wh—? How is that possible?' He was stunned for a moment then asked, 'When did you last see your husband?'

'Twenty-six years ago.'

'I'm sorry—what?' Elliot dropped her hands and took a few steps back, looking at her as though she had gone quite crazy. There was nothing for her to do now but to tell him her sorrow-filled story, but she also knew, as soon as he knew the truth about her past, it would change everything between them.

Sunainah's heart yearned to live in this moment, for

time to stand still, for hope to burn brightly between her and Elliot, the hope that they would forget everything and move forward with making a new life together. She already loved his children very much and perhaps, if she was very fortunate, he would allow her still to spend time with them.

Taking a deep breath, she nodded, gesturing to the chair on the other side of her desk. 'Would you like to sit down?'

Elliot turned his head sharply, staring at the chair as though he hadn't realised it was there.

'Trying to put some physical distance between us?'

She shrugged one shoulder. 'Perhaps.'

Elliot nodded once and walked to the chair, but to her surprise he picked it up and carried it around to her side of the desk, putting it directly opposite her own chair. 'I don't like barriers, Sunainah. I've had to hurdle and navigate my way around them quite a bit over the past few years. I don't like them and I refuse to have them erected between the two of us. Not now. Not after that amazing kiss.' He sat on the chair and looked up at her. 'Ready when you are.'

Sunainah lowered herself onto her own chair and calmly folded her hands in her lap. She would play it his way for now but she knew what would happen. It had happened before with Raj. When he had discovered the truth about her marriage, he had been disgusted, calling her 'damaged goods'. Well, she had survived one rejection. She could survive another.

Squaring her shoulders, Sunainah forced herself to meet Elliot's eyes. She did not want to see the moment he recoiled from her but she knew she had to so that she could start to heal her heart and eventually move forward with her life.

'When I was a teenager my mother became very ill. She was in and out of hospital a lot. My father was a university lecturer and he took time off work to nurse her, to be by her side. We moved towns so she could get better treatment but during this process I started to miss a lot of school and sometimes, when my mother was hospitalised, my father would stay there, leaving me alone to fend for myself. I do not blame him,' she said quickly. 'He simply lost track of time and he was always most apologetic when he finally came home.

'Because my mother was ill, my father had made contact with her estranged family. They had cut her off as dead when she had defied my grandfather and chosen to marry an Englishman, rather than the marriage they had arranged.'

'But they were happy? Your parents?'

Sunainah smiled. 'Very. Still, much to my father's surprise, my grandfather was very concerned and even visited my mother in hospital. He was very traditional and to forgive her was a huge step for him. Both my parents were delighted with this reconciliation so when my grandfather offered to have me come and stay at his family home so I was not left alone, they immediately accepted.'

Elliot raised an eyebrow. 'You went to stay with them?'

She closed her eyes and nodded. 'For six months.'

'What?'

She opened her eyes again, desperate for him to understand. 'My mother was very ill and my father needed to be by her side, to care for her. Surely you can understand that.'

Elliot hung his head and nodded. 'I do, but six months?'

'I was a teenager, not a little girl like Daphne. My father would send me weekly letters, giving me updates on my mother's progress, and I would write back, telling them about my life at Grandfather's house.'

Sunainah paused for a moment, trying to ignore the racing of her heart, the dryness in her mouth as she forced herself to relive the darkest part of her life. She owed Elliot that much at least.

'My grandfather's house was a busy place, with my mother's two sisters, their husbands and young children living there as well. He owned a farm and his good friend, Amir, owned the farm next to his. My grandfather had unfortunately had a bad year with his crops but Amir had done well.'

Sunainah squeezed her hands tighter together, needing to keep her voice calm and controlled as she spoke the next words. 'Amir offered to assist my grandfather but there were…conditions.' She paused again, desperate to control the rising emotion that was threatening to choke her, to stop her talking, but she forced the words calmly past her lips.

'You see, my mother had been promised in marriage to Amir many years before and when she defied my grandfather, there was friction between the two men.'

Elliot's eyes widened with dawning realisation. 'No.' He shook his head. 'No. Don't say that they—'

'My grandfather arranged for me to be wed to Amir.'

'When you were fourteen!'

'The marriage would save my grandfather's farm

and Amir would finally get the wife my grandfather had promised him.'

'But you were *fourteen*!'

'Life is different in some parts of India, Elliot. Many girls are wed at such an age.'

'How old was Amir?'

'Thirty-five.'

'What!' Elliot stood and turned away from her, pacing around the room as he digested this news. Sunainah closed her eyes and raised a trembling hand to her lips. She had expected a reaction like this. The disbelief, the disgrace, the disgust. Elliot's reaction was the same as Raj's had been.

'The marriage was never consummated,' she offered quickly, desperation in her tone, eager to have him understand that she was not really damaged goods. 'It was a condition of the arrangement that I was not to become Amir's wife in every sense of the word until I was sixteen and legally a woman.'

Elliot spun back to face her. 'And your father permitted this?'

'I did write to him. I told him everything but, I discovered later, my grandfather had not been posting my letters. My father's letters became more sporadic as well and whenever I asked if my grandmother had any new news on my mother's health, she would simply tell me that there had been no change.'

'How long did you live with Amir?'

'Seven weeks—but nothing romantic happened between us.' She shook her head, her eyes imploring him to believe her. 'I did the cooking and the cleaning and the washing. Looked after the house and did farm chores. That is all. I promise.'

'So how did you…get out? How did you leave?' El-liot's hands were clenched into fists, his words spoken between gritted teeth. Sunainah tried to hold back her tears, wishing she had been stronger, that she had been less trusting, that she had been more like her mother, who had not only stood up to her domineering father but had defied him by marrying the man of her own choosing.

'My father came. He just turned up one evening as I was finishing the dishes. He burst into Amir's house and punched him in the face. His eyes were blazing with a fire I had never seen before. He was very angry. He told me to get into the car and as soon as I was safe inside, he drove away. I did not know where we were going or what my grandfather might think or anything. My father did not speak to me and when we arrived back at the hospital, where my mother was very much improved in health, they both held me and just…cried.'

Silent tears ran down Sunainah's cheeks as she looked blankly in front of her, her words recalling the scene as though she was speaking of someone else's life. 'Ten days later, we were on our way to England. We never went back to India.'

'Good.' There was great vehemence in the word. 'Why didn't your father seek an annulment of the mar-riage?' Elliot's tone was brisk and businesslike, not at all tender and comforting, as it had been before. Sunainah tried to control the pain in her heart, feeling him dis-tance himself from her already.

Sunainah brushed the tears from her cheeks. 'I thought he had. He told me he would take care of it.'

Elliot frowned, shoving his hands into his pockets. 'How did you find out he hadn't?'

Sunainah looked away from him, down to her lap. She had come this far. It seemed ridiculous not to continue. 'About five years ago I met a man—Rajesh. I was living in Sydney, completing my paediatric training, and he was a brilliant young Indian neurosurgeon. We started dating and soon we were engaged to be married. His mother approved of the match and I truly thought Raj loved me.'

Elliot nodded slowly, his clever mind computing the next bit of information. 'You couldn't find the document stating you were divorced.'

'No.' She shook her head, her hair swishing around her shoulders. 'After I had told Raj of...of what my grandfather had organised, he was naturally surprised but told me he would look into things. I had assured him the marriage had not been consummated and at the time he told me he believed me.'

'And later?'

'He called the wedding off. He told me I should have stayed with Amir, that I had been legally wed to the man in a traditional arrangement and it needed to be honoured.'

'That's...' He shook his head. 'How could...?' He closed his mouth, as though trying to comprehend everything she was telling him.

She continued, 'At that time, my father's dementia had become worse and while Raj was very traditional in many respects, when it came to having a sick father-in-law living with us after our marriage, he was very modern, insisting my father be put into a nursing home.'

'What?' Elliot stared at her from across the room, his arms spread wide. 'What is it with the men in your life? Did none of them take care of you?'

Sunainah stood from her chair at his words, a flash of fire burning through her. 'I can take care of myself now. When Raj left, I decided it was time I took control over my life. My father and I moved here from Sydney at my instigation. The sunshine was better for his health and there were new treatments for dementia being trialled. My friends were here for support when I needed it and now I have the position of head of the paediatric ward at a busy teaching hospital.'

'I'm not saying you *can't* look after yourself, Sunainah. It's quite clear that you can.' Elliot took a step towards her but stopped. 'I just meant, speaking as the father of a little girl, that it's a father's duty to protect his daughter, to teach her how to protect herself, how to be strong, how to become an independent woman. I'm all for girl power and I intend to empower Daphne as best as I can, but I also want her to know that I am there for her, whenever she needs me—no matter what.'

'You are criticising my father now? Saying he did not take good care of me?'

'Sunainah, you ended up in an arranged marriage— at the age of fourteen!'

'But he rescued me in the end and, besides, he needed to be there for my mother, to be by her side. He had thought I was safe, just as you thought Daphne was safe with your wife's parents, and when you realised what was happening, how they were taking over and controlling the major decisions in Daphne's life, you stepped in and rescued her.'

Elliot opened his mouth to speak but closed it again.

'It is the same thing. Different degrees of circumstance and emotion but the point is you are there for your daughter now.' She nodded. 'You are stronger than my own father. He admitted his weakness to me and not long before he died. In a rare moment of clarity he apologised for not protecting me. He could not think of the incident without feeling immense shame and he asked for my forgiveness.'

'So why didn't he get the annulment? Why didn't he take care of it?'

'He thought he had. He had filed papers but Amir had refused to sign them. Then my mother passed away, finally succumbing to the illness she had been fighting for many years. We grieved together and when my father suggested moving to Australia, for the two of us to begin a brand-new life together, wipe the slate clean, we did just that. I think he thought he had continued with the pursuit of the annulment but as time went on and our wounds started to heal, it seemed to fade into the background of our lives…as though it had all happened to someone else.'

'A new beginning.'

'Yes.'

'I understand that.'

'I thought you would.'

She wanted so much for him to come to her, to cross the room, to haul her close into her arms as he had done when he had first entered her office. To hold her. To kiss her. To tell her everything would be all right. But she knew it could not be the way things would progress. She was not a free woman and Elliot deserved better. He did need a new start, not only for himself but for his children, and she would not stand in the way of his chance to find happiness.

'But why, when you discovered you were still married to Amir, why didn't *you* file the papers again?'

Sunainah shook her head. 'To get Amir to sign the papers, I would need to see him. I had tried to do it through lawyers but every time Amir refused, saying he would only sign if I brought the papers myself.' She hung her head as a wave of shame washed over her.

'I...I have done so much. I have come so far. I have taken control over my life, I have looked after my father, and after many years of being sick he passed away only a few short months ago. Every day I have to remind myself that I have no other family, that I am all alone. I am simply not strong enough to go to India, to face Amir.' She choked off her words, biting her lip to control the powerful wave of tears she was desperately trying to hold at bay. 'I cannot,' she whispered.

'Well, then.' Elliot's words were firm and held a hint of finality. Sunainah closed her eyes, unable to look at him, unable to see the way he would be looking at her with disgust. She was not worthy of a man like him and as she could not bring herself to seek an annulment, it meant there was no possible way the two of them would ever be together. 'I guess that's all there is to it.'

At his words, Sunainah gasped in pain, unable to hold back the flood any longer, and with her heart breaking in utter despair she fled from her office.

Away from her past. Away from her present. Away from the possibility of a future with Elliot.

CHAPTER TEN

SUNAINAH SAT IN the corner of her darkened house, behind the furniture, hugging her knees close to her chest. Around her neck was the colourful button necklace Daphne had lovingly made her, and she could not help but rub her fingers over the smooth surfaces, wishing with all her heart that things could have turned out differently. She could not believe she had not only spoken openly to Elliot about her past but that he had rejected her, just as she had been sure he would.

The little voice inside her head kept spinning around and around, telling her she would always be alone, she would never find anyone to love her unconditionally, that she was indeed damaged.

Her cowardice, her inability to face Amir had caused her unhappiness yet again. The pain and anguish pulsing through Sunainah's body caused a fresh batch of tears to trickle down her cheeks. How she wished Elliot had been able to accept her for who she was, warts and all, to know she was not as strong as she might appear. There was nothing she could do to go back and change her past, but she had to figure out a way to live with her present.

It was very cruel that the instant she had realised she

was one hundred percent in love with Elliot had been the moment he had looked into her eyes and said the words that had caused her heart to break.

I guess that's all there is to it.

He had given up. He had finally realised she was not worth fighting for. He might even believe the worst of her, as Raj had. A fresh batch of tears welled up and spilled over her lashes as the pain in her heart continued to paralyse her. Never before had she felt such a deep and abiding emotion, one filled with regret, with fear and yet overshadowed by a perfect love…a love that could never be.

After racing from her office, she had left the ward, heading into the stairwell and going down, down as far as she could, her feet carrying her away from that piercing look in his wonderful blue eyes, eyes that would never again look at her in the same way. Elliot could never love someone like her, have her be a mother to his wonderful children.

At the bottom of the stairwell she had stopped, unable to go any lower.

There, in the basement stairwell, she had crouched down and allowed the tears to flow. She had felt small, useless and insignificant. Regret at what might have been pulsed through her as the tears had run silently down her cheeks. She had pulled a handkerchief from her pocket and held it to her eyes, desperate not to make a sound, even though her heart had been breaking.

She loved Elliot. Truly loved him with every fibre of her being. This was not the same emotion she had experienced with Raj. This was different, more powerful, more consuming, and it made it all the more painful to know they could never be together.

How could she have not realised that sooner? But even if she had, there was still no way she could have prevented him from finding out the truth. She had tried to put up road blocks, had tried to keep him at a distance because he deserved to find his new beginning, his new happiness with his children, especially after what he had shared with her. Losing his wife. Enduring a legal battle for his children. Yes, he deserved a world of happiness, which was why it was imperative for her to leave him alone.

Yet even the thought of working alongside him every day, loving him the way she did but needing to let him go, had brought a fresh round of sorrow.

'Sunainah?'

At the sound of her name, she froze.

'Sunainah?'

It had been Reggie's voice. Sunainah had breathed again, listening as her friend's footsteps kept descending in the stairwell. 'Reggie?'

'There you are.' Reggie sighed with relief as she quickened her pace and within the next instant had pulled Sunainah into her arms. 'Elliot was worried about you.'

'I doubt that.' Sunainah's words were filled with dejection. 'I told him, Reggie. About my past.'

'Ah. Well, now, that makes more sense.'

'What does?' Sunainah stood and brushed her clothes down before blowing her nose.

'Nothing.' Reggie shook her head then looked at her friend with a hint of concern. 'Listen, why don't you head home? Try and get some sleep.'

'That is not going to happen. I have too much to do

here, and besides, with the way I am feeling right now, I doubt there is the remotest possibility that I will sleep.'

'Then rest, sit in a corner, rock back and forth, wallow in self-pity. It doesn't matter, Sunainah. Just leave the hospital. Nicole told me you've been in since very early this morning and to make a long day worse, there's been this weird German epidemic thing sweeping the State.' Reggie brushed Sunainah's hair back behind her ears. 'Everyone's emotions have been running on high voltage.' She smiled tenderly at her friend. 'Some more than others.'

Sunainah looked closely at her friend. 'What does that mean?'

'It means you not only had your usual work to contend with but were also trying to figure out the treatment for your patients.'

'E-Elliot was the one who remembered the symptoms.'

'It doesn't matter now.'

Sunainah saw that Reggie had not missed the way she had tripped over saying Elliot's name out loud. How was she supposed to cope, working alongside him every day, when just saying his name was already painful? Would it ever get any easier?

'You've helped everyone,' Reggie continued. 'Your patients are stable and people you trust are working in the ward this evening so it's time for you to head home. You always put everyone else ahead of yourself, Sunainah.' Reggie looked closely at her friend. 'It's your superpower, honey. You give and you give and you just keep on giving, no matter how much you might be hurting inside.'

'My superpower?'

Reggie shrugged, a bright, beaming smile touching her lips. 'It's a thing. Everyone wants to figure out their superpower.'

'I am guessing yours is cheering people up? Being forever the optimist?'

'Ta-dah!' Reggie spread her arms wide, her eyes twinkling with delight. 'You know me too well, which means you'll also know I mean it when I say it's time for you to go home and rest.'

The smile slid from Sunainah's face, and she shook her head. 'I do not have my car here because I came to the hospital with E—with my neighbour and his sick little son.'

'So I gathered.'

'I should at least check on Joshua but—'

'Let it go, Sunainah.' Reggie angled her head towards the stairs, and when Sunainah nodded the two of them started walking up. 'Elli—uh, the staff told me young Joshua is doing extremely well, that he's definitely going to make a full recovery, so that's super good news. Now, as far as your transportation issues are concerned…' Reggie fished in her pocket for a moment and pulled out a set of car keys. 'Take my car. I'll be here all night long and you can bring it back in the morning when I've finished my shift.'

Sunainah stopped on a stair and leaned over to hug Reggie. 'Thank you. You are a good friend.'

'No.' Reggie held a finger up towards her. 'I am a *brilliant* friend.

'Who is not given to hyperbole at all,' she added, a smile touching her lips once more. Cheering people up really was Reggie's 'superpower'. Sunainah sighed. 'Thanks, Reggie.'

'I'll ensure your office is locked up and there's no drama about getting into your house because Mackenzie has a spare set of keys. Just go, Sunainah. You need time to think things through.'

And Reggie had been right. Sitting in the corner of her lounge room, allowing herself to wallow in self-pity, Sunainah somehow felt she was finally getting some sort of control over her confused thoughts. Her past was the problem but there was no changing it. How she had wished many times over the years that she could stand up to Amir, to claim the freedom that was rightfully hers?

Even thinking about what might happen, about what Amir might say or do, caused fear to lodge in her throat and her body to tremble. The darkness that had consumed her at the time, of living in the house with a man older than her father, of being so unsure of exactly what was happening, of wondering if her parents had forgotten all about her, the feelings of rejection and dejection instantly returned.

The darkness started to choke her. Now that she had opened that door, the emotions seemed to come flooding out, but then she thought about Elliot, about Daphne and Joshua. Of the times they had spent together, of the way the children had climbed onto her lap and snuggled into her arms.

The thoughts of them, of the three people she truly loved, brought a stream of pure light into the darkness that had engulfed her life for far too long. She held Daphne's button necklace close to her heart, hoping to stave off the repressive thoughts.

Sunainah lifted her head and opened her eyes. Perhaps, if she found the strength now, she could go to

India, face Amir once and for all and get him to sign the annulment papers. If she did that, she would be able to be with Elliot—if he still wanted her. Hope began to flare. Elliot was worth it. She would be strong for him, for Daphne and for Joshua.

'I can do this.' As she spoke the words out loud Sunainah felt as though a weight was being lifted from her shoulders. All she had to do was to focus on the wonderful memories she had created with Elliot and his children. She promised herself to think about only the good times because those were the memories that would propel her forward and maybe, just maybe, if she was able to take care of her past once and for all, there might be the smallest spark of hope that Elliot might one day come to care for her again.

Was it possible? Dared she dream of such a future?

She blew her nose one last time, a flood of optimism starting to clear her foggy mind. She would do this. She would be strong. She would not let anyone stop her from achieving her goal of freedom, of never again having to think about her past with shame.

She could do this. She could face her past. She *had* to do this if there was any chance she might one day be with Elliot. That was what she wanted more than anything in the world, to become a part of his life, a part of his family, a part of his new beginning.

Sunainah had just stood when she heard footsteps outside her door, followed a moment later by loud knocking. Her eyes widened at the sound and she gasped when she heard Elliot calling her name.

'Sunainah! Open up.'

He was here? Elliot was *here*? Her heart hammered wildly in terrified happiness. She was delighted to see him, that he was here, that he had sought her out, but she was deeply concerned with what he might want to say to her. Although, if he mentioned her past, she could now proudly tell him she was going to do everything she could to ensure she would be completely free in the future. She wanted him to know just how important he and his children were to her and if he…if he did not want her after that, then at least she could be satisfied she had done everything possible. Then she could move on with her life, free from any shackles of the past.

'Sunainah! Open the door. Please? It's important.'

There was a mild hint of panic in his tone and for one fleeting second her mind cleared of all her selfish reasons for wanting him there and switched into concerned doctor mode.

'Is it Joshua?' She rushed to the door, opening it with a worried look on her face. 'Is Joshua all right? Has his temperature spiked again?'

All the urgency seemed to melt from Elliot as he stood at her door, staring at her in wonderment. There she was. *His* Sunainah. Dressed in a comfortable pair of jeans, a large T-shirt, her glorious hair still loose and Daphne's button necklace around her neck. Elliot was overcome by her natural beauty, and it was ridiculous to even try and stop the way his heart pounded at the sight of her. 'Joshua is doing very well, as are all the other patients.'

'Well, I am pleased to hear that.' She was finding it increasingly difficult not to stare at him. He was so incredibly handsome with his dark hair and straight nose and blue eyes and perfect lips that fitted perfectly with her own.

'You are?'

'Yes. Joshua's health is important to me…Daphne's, too.' Her words were soft, spoken as though in a daze as she continued to drink in the sight of him.

Elliot stared back at her. 'What about *my* health? Are you concerned about that, Sunainah?'

It was only then that she lowered her eyes, just for a moment, before she looked at him, fair and square. 'Yes, Elliot.'

At her answer he stepped forward, closing the distance between them, and pressed a hard kiss to her mouth, startling her. 'Then please don't ever run out on me like that again.'

'Uh…' Sunainah blinked rapidly, trying to figure out what had just happened. Elliot sidestepped her, coming into her home, and when she continued to just stand there, completely stunned by the hot and heavy kiss, he closed the front door for her and took her hand in his.

'Where did you go? I looked for you but I… You seemed to disappear into thin air. I ran into Reggie and—'

'You were *really* worried?'

'Of course I was. You were upset and crying and it must have been so difficult for you to tell me about your past and then you were just—gone.' He spread his hands wide. 'Why would you think I wouldn't be worried about you?'

'Because…you said that was all there was to it, that you wanted nothing more to do with me, and—'

'Whoa. Whoa, there.' Elliot stared at her for a moment then shook his head. 'You thought, after everything you had just told me, that I wanted nothing more to do with you? *That's* why you ran out?'

'Yes.'

'I thought you ran out because you were upset, not because of what I said.'

'But...' She frowned at him, even more confused than before. 'You said—that was all there was to it.'

'That's right.' Elliot stepped a little closer and rested a hand on her shoulder, his thumb gently caressing her. 'I wasn't going to let you live the rest of your life wondering whether or not you were still married to some old man who should have known better than to take a child bride—conditions or no conditions.'

'It is different in some parts of Indi—'

'I don't care.' His words were strong, vehement and filled with power, yet his touch on her shoulders was soft, reassuring and caring. Add that to the way he had kissed her and was now looking intently into her eyes and Sunainah started to wonder whether she had not done Elliot a great disservice.

'I want to help you, Sunainah. My brother is a lawyer in Melbourne and I can call him tomorrow to ask his help in putting the wheels in motion. I will also fly to India with you, stand by your side while that man signs the forms declaring the marriage null and void.'

She blinked a few times, trying to comprehend his words, unable to believe what she was hearing. 'You would...do that...for me?'

Elliot's lip twitched into a smile as he came closer, cupping her face. 'Well, I do have my own selfish reasons.'

'You do?' His words only confused her even more.

'Sunainah, I don't want you to be married to any man—except me. Getting this whole situation—one that never should have taken place in the beginning—

sorted out so that we can be together is of paramount importance. You deserve a world of happiness, Sunainah, and I am the man who is going to give it to you.'

'You are?'

His smile was gorgeous and glorious and absolutely perfect. 'You're a highly intelligent woman who is responsible for running a busy children's department in an equally busy teaching hospital.' He bent and brushed a very quick kiss across her lips.

'You are no longer an unempowered fourteen-year-old girl. You are strong and wonderful and awesome and you fit perfectly into my arms and when you kiss me...' Elliot groaned with remembered delight. 'You set me on fire. You do realise that, don't you?'

Sunainah looked up at him, unable to believe he was saying such wonderful things to her. Had she finally found a man who was really going to look after her, be there for her, no matter what? He was going to fight for her, fight alongside her to ensure she was free to marry hi—

'Wait a moment.' Sunainah eased back a little so she could look at him more carefully. 'Did you just say you wanted to...marry me?'

Elliot laughed and smiled down into her upturned face. 'Yes.'

'Are...are you sure?' There was concern in her eyes as she watched his expression as closely as she could. 'I know you moved here to make a new beginning for you and the children. I do not want to get in the way of that happening. Your first priority—' Her words were interrupted by Elliot's lips pressing against hers, effectively silencing her.

'There,' he said a moment later. 'Now, just remain

quiet for a moment longer, please. I want to ask you to marry me so that there are absolutely no doubts as to my intentions.'

Sunainah did as he asked but after brushing one more glorious kiss to her lips, Elliot eased back slightly then took her hands in his and then surprised her even further by dropping down to one knee.

'Elliot!'

'Shh.' He smiled up at her. 'Sunainah Carrington— Wait…do you have a middle name? I cannot believe how little I know about you.' He shook his head in bemusement. 'At least we have the rest of our lives to find out. Anyway, I'm getting sidetracked.' He paused and made sure he was looking deeply into her eyes.

'What I *do* know, Sunainah, is that I have come to feel so lost when you're not around me, so discombobulated when we're apart and so powerless that when I think of my life without you in it I don't seem to function at all. I need you, Sunainah, and I realise I come as a package deal but rest assured that my children adore you.'

Sunainah smiled, her eyes filling once more but this time with happy tears, unable to believe Elliot was saying such wonderful things. 'I adore them, too.' She touched a hand to her button necklace as she said the words and her reward was a loving smile from the man of her dreams.

'Most importantly, I love you. I love you with all my heart and I would be the happiest man alive if you would agree to marry me.'

'Elliot?' Sunainah tugged at his hands and he immediately stood, slipping his arms around her waist while she linked hers around his neck, the two of them wanting to be as close as possible. 'Are you sure we can sort everything out?'

'Absolutely positive.' He pressed a quick kiss to her cheek.

'And the children? Are you sure they will not mind having a new mother?'

'Mind?' He kissed her other cheek. 'You're all they talk about.'

Sunainah bit her lip.

'Any other questions? I want to have any and all necessary questions answered. I want your mind to be at rest so we can move forward and start our new life together.'

'A new beginning?'

'Is that a yes?'

Sunainah nodded. 'That is a yes. I love you so much, Elliot. I never believed I could ever be this happy.'

Elliot's smiled increased as he lowered his head, desperate to capture her lips in a heart-warming kiss that would begin the rest of their lives together.

'To new beginnings,' he murmured, just before he kissed his new fiancée for the first time.

EPILOGUE

'I STILL CAN'T believe you actually walked into Amir's house, slapped the papers onto the table and demanded he sign them.' Reggie shook her head, a wide grin on her lips as she placed the wreath of flowers onto Sunainah's dark hair.

'Elliot told me all he had to do was stand at the door, that you were all power and fire and Amir took one look at you and almost cowered with fear,' Bergan added.

'That's our Sunainah,' Mackenzie agreed.

Sunainah sighed with happiness and looked at her friends. 'I am free. Free from all that oppression, free to start a new life with the man of my dreams.' Even just thinking about Elliot, the man who would soon become her husband, brought a lightness to her heart and smile to her lips.

'I love it that you chose to have a garden wedding,' Mackenzie said as she touched up Sunainah's make-up. There would be no traditional ceremony for her. Elliot had been right when he had said this was a new beginning and as such, having an informal gathering of their closest friends was definitely the way to go.

They were all in a marquee that had been set aside purely for the bride to finish her preparations before stepping out to walk down an aisle of rose petals, dutifully thrown by her two flower girls, Daphne and Ruthie, towards her impatient fiancé.

'Come on, girls,' Reggie said to the two little ones, after she'd finished securing Sunainah's flowers to her hair. 'Let's get these lovely flowers on your heads and then you can look just as pretty as the bride.'

'Yay.' Daphne clapped her hands and climbed up onto Sunainah's lap, hugging her new mother-to-be tightly. Sunainah smiled and hugged her new daughter-to-be back, kissing the top of her head. 'I like looking like you, Mummy.' The little girl giggled as she said the word. 'Mummy...' Daphne shrugged her shoulders and giggled again. 'I like it.'

'So do I,' Sunainah replied.

Within another five minutes they were all ready to go. Everyone wore flat ballet slippers, the three bridesmaids Mackenzie, Bergan and Reggie all dressed in different pastel-coloured, calf-length dresses that floated and fluttered.

'I'll look after Daphne. I know what to do,' Ruthie told Sunainah with great authority. 'I've already been a flower girl twice.' She held up two fingers and grinned.

'Only one more to go,' Mackenzie said in a singsong voice as they all turned to look at Reggie.

'What?' Reggie laughed at her friends. 'As if I could ever find the man who could keep up with me. Besides, flirting is far too much fun.' She winked at the three of them and struck a cheeky pose, making them all laugh.

'Reggie. Please do not ever change,' Sunainah said as she picked up her simple bouquet of wild flowers. 'For now...I do not want to be late. My two favourite men are waiting for me.'

'No doubt impatiently,' Bergan added, as she gave the signal for the musicians to start playing.

As the light music floated around them and her friends walked down the aisle in front of her, Ruthie and Daphne throwing their rose petals, Sunainah looked towards the other end where Elliot stood, Joshua securely in his arms, impatiently awaiting for her arrival.

Elliot turned to look at her and gasped with delight. Sunainah smiled brightly at the love of her life, pleased her face was not hidden beneath a veil. She wanted Elliot to know exactly how happy she was. More happy than she had ever been in her life...thanks to her new family.

* * * * *

Mills & Boon® Hardback

October 2013

ROMANCE

The Greek's Marriage Bargain	Sharon Kendrick
An Enticing Debt to Pay	Annie West
The Playboy of Puerto Banús	Carol Marinelli
Marriage Made of Secrets	Maya Blake
Never Underestimate a Caffarelli	Melanie Milburne
The Divorce Party	Jennifer Hayward
A Hint of Scandal	Tara Pammi
A Façade to Shatter	Lynn Raye Harris
Whose Bed Is It Anyway?	Natalie Anderson
Last Groom Standing	Kimberly Lang
Single Dad's Christmas Miracle	Susan Meier
Snowbound with the Soldier	Jennifer Faye
The Redemption of Rico D'Angelo	Michelle Douglas
The Christmas Baby Surprise	Shirley Jump
Backstage with Her Ex	Louisa George
Blame It on the Champagne	Nina Harrington
Christmas Magic in Heatherdale	Abigail Gordon
The Motherhood Mix-Up	Jennifer Taylor

MEDICAL

Gold Coast Angels: A Doctor's Redemption	Marion Lennox
Gold Coast Angels: Two Tiny Heartbeats	Fiona McArthur
The Secret Between Them	Lucy Clark
Craving Her Rough Diamond Doc	Amalie Berlin

Mills & Boon® Large Print
October 2013

ROMANCE

The Sheikh's Prize	Lynne Graham
Forgiven but not Forgotten?	Abby Green
His Final Bargain	Melanie Milburne
A Throne for the Taking	Kate Walker
Diamond in the Desert	Susan Stephens
A Greek Escape	Elizabeth Power
Princess in the Iron Mask	Victoria Parker
The Man Behind the Pinstripes	Melissa McClone
Falling for the Rebel Falcon	Lucy Gordon
Too Close for Comfort	Heidi Rice
The First Crush Is the Deepest	Nina Harrington

HISTORICAL

Reforming the Viscount	Annie Burrows
A Reputation for Notoriety	Diane Gaston
The Substitute Countess	Lyn Stone
The Sword Dancer	Jeannie Lin
His Lady of Castlemora	Joanna Fulford

MEDICAL

NYC Angels: Unmasking Dr Serious	Laura Iding
NYC Angels: The Wallflower's Secret	Susan Carlisle
Cinderella of Harley Street	Anne Fraser
You, Me and a Family	Sue MacKay
Their Most Forbidden Fling	Melanie Milburne
The Last Doctor She Should Ever Date	Louisa George

0913 GEN STD LP

ROMANCE

MEDICAL

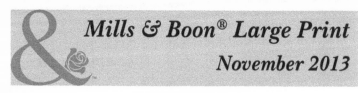

Mills & Boon® Large Print
November 2013

ROMANCE

His Most Exquisite Conquest	Emma Darcy
One Night Heir	Lucy Monroe
His Brand of Passion	Kate Hewitt
The Return of Her Past	Lindsay Armstrong
The Couple who Fooled the World	Maisey Yates
Proof of Their Sin	Dani Collins
In Petrakis's Power	Maggie Cox
A Cowboy To Come Home To	Donna Alward
How to Melt a Frozen Heart	Cara Colter
The Cattleman's Ready-Made Family	Michelle Douglas
What the Paparazzi Didn't See	Nicola Marsh

HISTORICAL

Mistress to the Marquis	Margaret McPhee
A Lady Risks All	Bronwyn Scott
Her Highland Protector	Ann Lethbridge
Lady Isobel's Champion	Carol Townend
No Role for a Gentleman	Gail Whitiker

MEDICAL

NYC Angels: Flirting with Danger	Tina Beckett
NYC Angels: Tempting Nurse Scarlet	Wendy S. Marcus
One Life Changing Moment	Lucy Clark
P.S. You're a Daddy!	Dianne Drake
Return of the Rebel Doctor	Joanna Neil
One Baby Step at a Time	Meredith Webber

1013 GEN STD LP